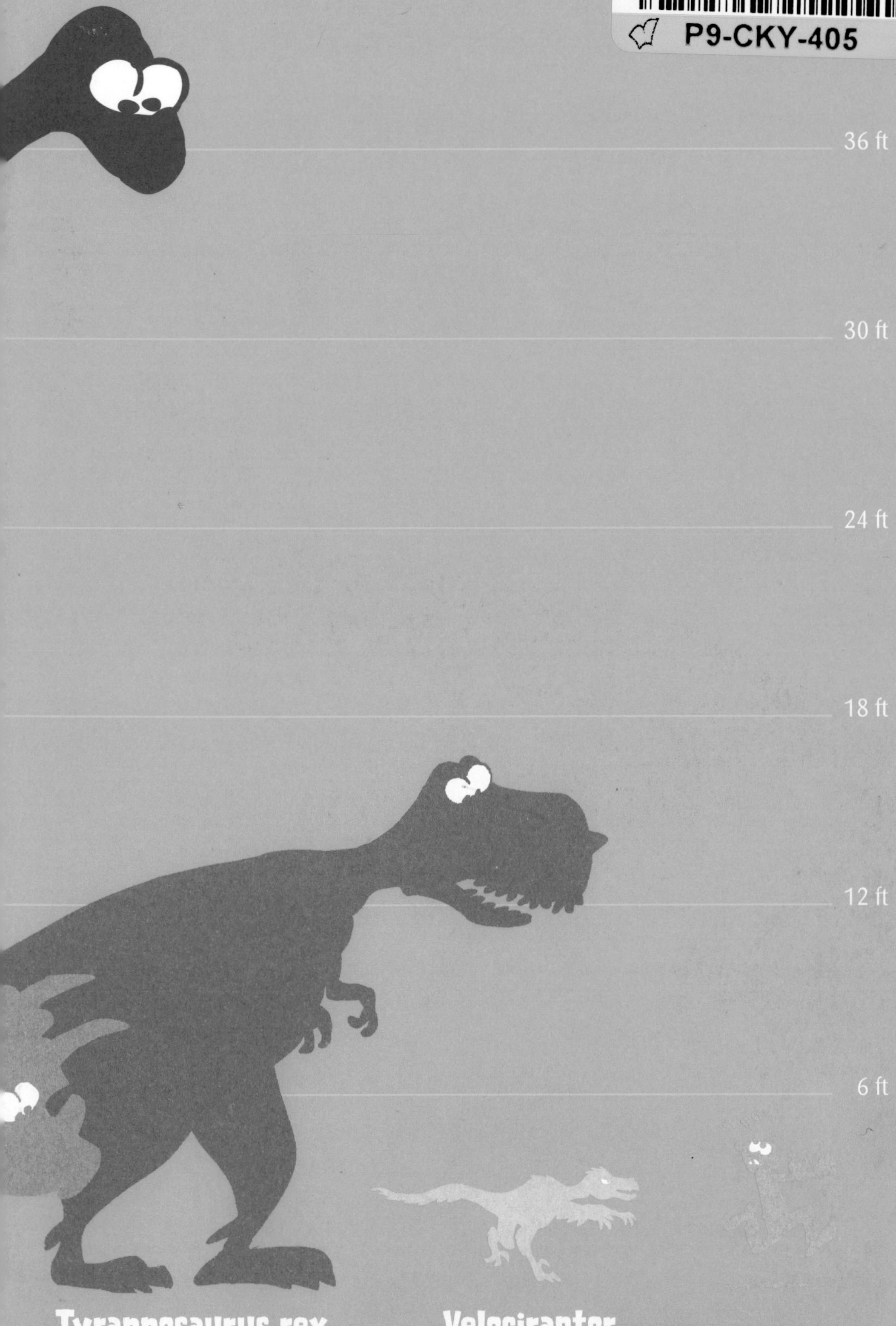
36 ft
30 ft
24 ft
18 ft
12 ft
6 ft
Tyrannosaurus rex
Velociraptor

Dinosaurs

YOU SHOULDN'T HAVE PICKED ON ME!

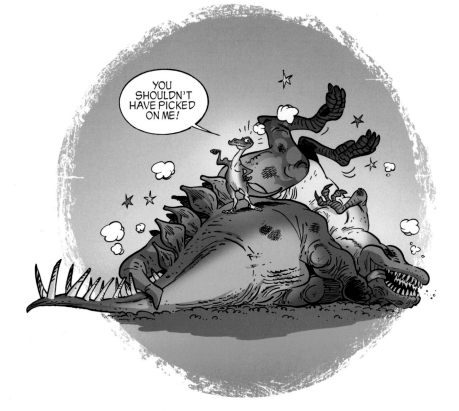

Bloz • Art
Arnaud Plumeri • Story
Maëla Cosson • Color

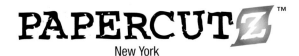

PAPERCUTZ™
New York

Dinosaurs Graphic Novels Available from PAPERCUTZ™

Graphic Novel #1
"In the Beginning…"

Graphic Novel #2
"Bite of the Albertosaurus"

Graphic Novel #3
"Jurassic Smarts"

Les Dinosaures [Dinosaurs] by Arnaud Plumeri & Bloz © 2011 BAMBOO ÉDITION.
www.bamboo.fr
All other editorial material © 2014 by Papercutz.

DINOSAURS #2
"Bite of the Albertosaurus"

Arnaud Plumeri – Writer
Bloz – Artist
Maëla Cosson – Colorist
Nanette McGuinness – Translation
Janice Chiang – Letterer
Bryce Gold – Editorial Intern
Beth Scorzato – Production Coordinator
Michael Petranek – Editor
Jim Salicrup
Editor-in-Chief

ISBN: 978-1-59707-515-2

Printed in China
August 2014 by WKT Co. LTD
3/F Phase I Leader Industrial Centre
188 Texaco Road, Tseun Wan, N.T., Hong Kong

Papercutz books may be purchased for business or promotional use.
For information on bulk purchases please contact Macmillan Corporate and Premium Sales Department at (800) 221-7945 x5442.

Distributed by Macmillan
Second Papercutz Printing

DINOSAURS graphic novels are available for $10.99 only in hardcover. Available from booksellers everywhere. You can also order online from papercutz.com Or call 1-800-886-1223, Monday through Friday, 9 – 5 EST. MC, Visa, and AmEx accepted. To order by mail, please add $4.00 for postage and handling for first book ordered, $1.00 for each additional book and make check payable to NBM Publishing. Send to: Papercutz, 160 Broadway, Suite 700, East Wing, New York, NY 10038.

DINOSAURS graphic novels are also available digitally wherever e-books are sold.

Papercutz.com

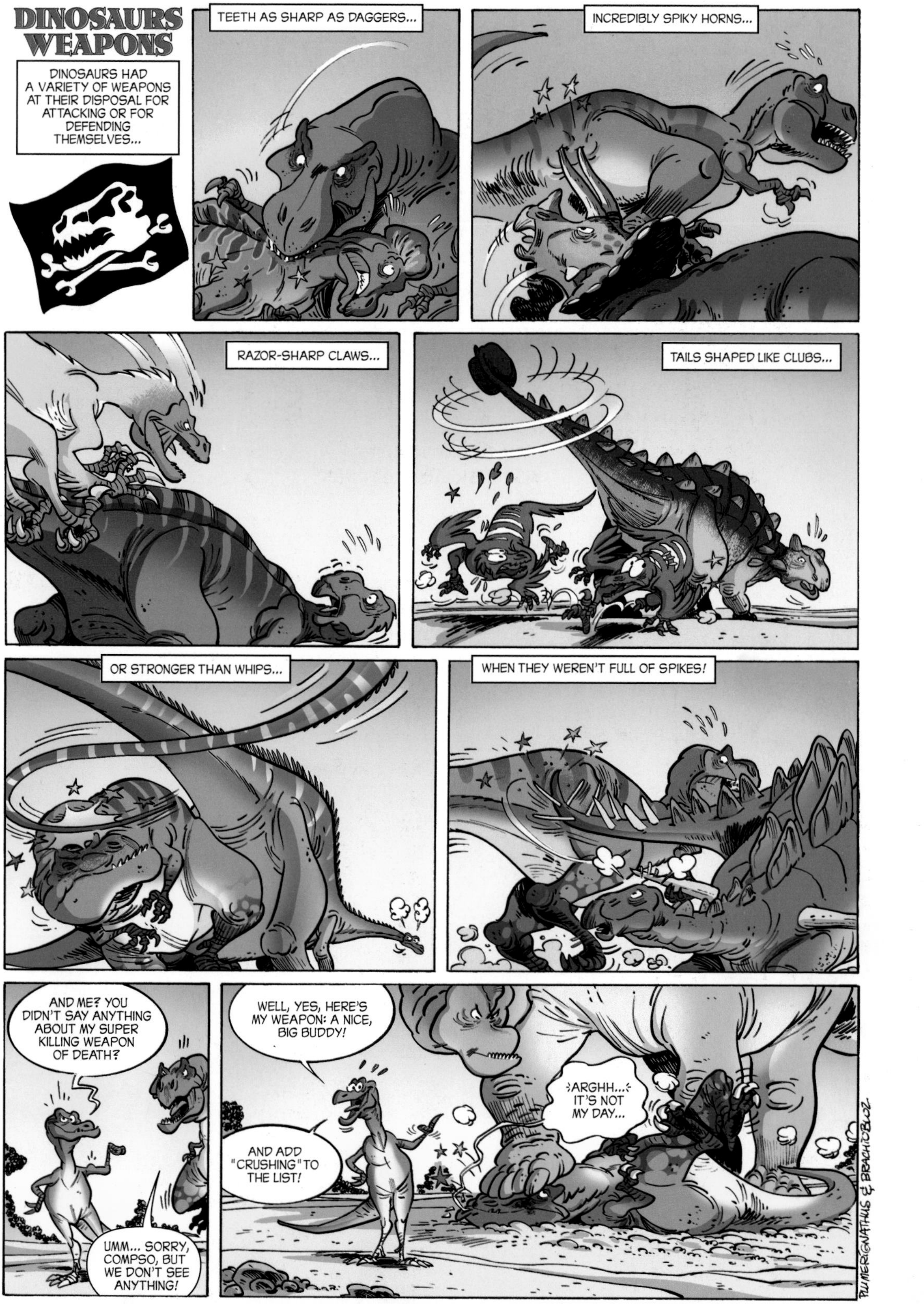
DINOSAURS WEAPONS
DINOSAURS HAD A VARIETY OF WEAPONS AT THEIR DISPOSAL FOR ATTACKING OR FOR DEFENDING THEMSELVES...
TEETH AS SHARP AS DAGGERS...
INCREDIBLY SPIKY HORNS...
RAZOR-SHARP CLAWS...
TAILS SHAPED LIKE CLUBS...
OR STRONGER THAN WHIPS...
WHEN THEY WEREN'T FULL OF SPIKES!
AND ME? YOU DIDN'T SAY ANYTHING ABOUT MY SUPER KILLING WEAPON OF DEATH?
UMM... SORRY, COMPSO, BUT WE DON'T SEE ANYTHING!
WELL, YES, HERE'S MY WEAPON: A NICE, BIG BUDDY!
AND ADD "CRUSHING" TO THE LIST!
ARGHH... IT'S NOT MY DAY...

THE HISTORY OF THE EARTH IN 24 HOURS

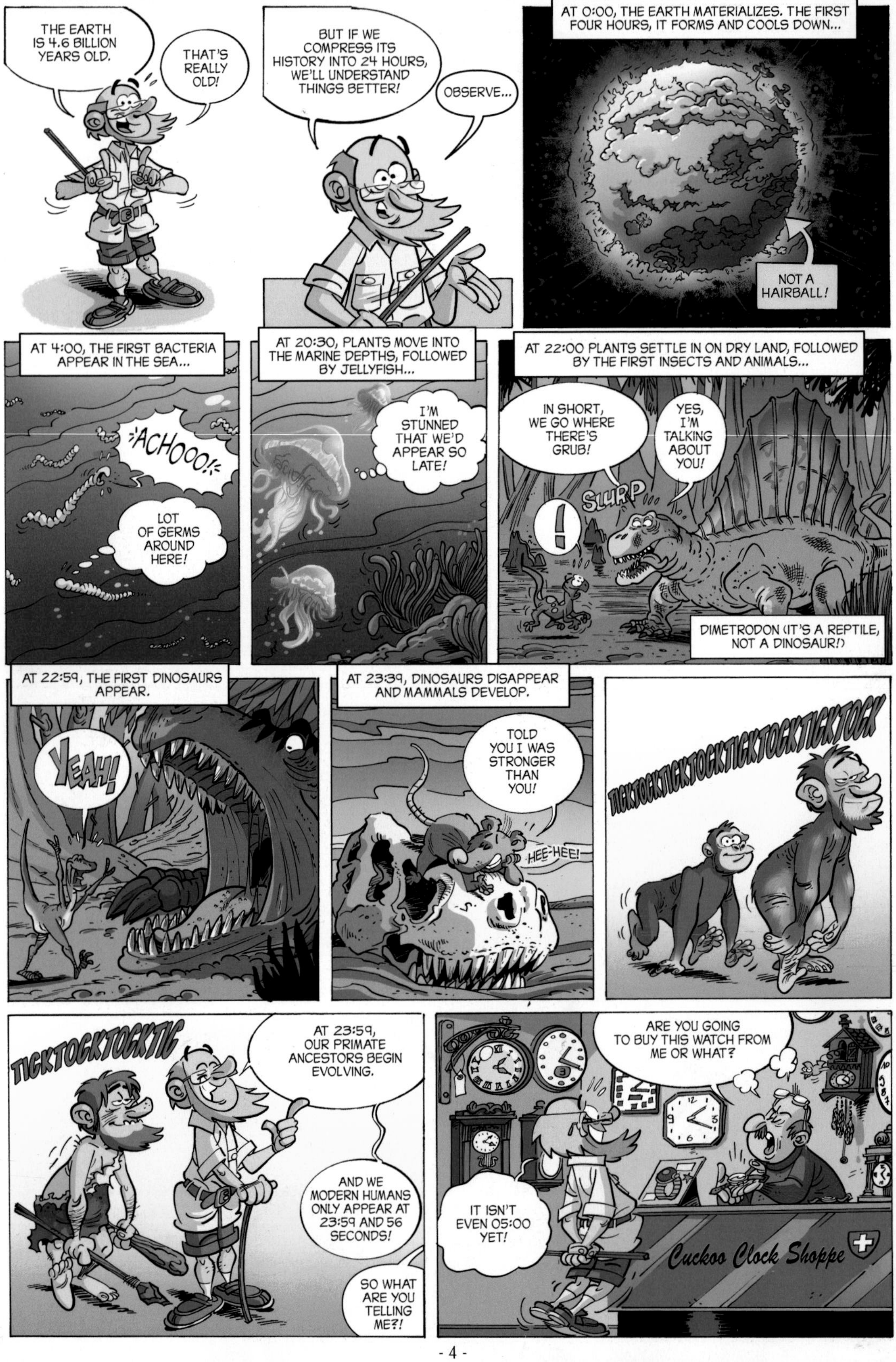

THE EARTH IS 4.6 BILLION YEARS OLD.
THAT'S REALLY OLD!
BUT IF WE COMPRESS ITS HISTORY INTO 24 HOURS, WE'LL UNDERSTAND THINGS BETTER!
OBSERVE...
AT 0:00, THE EARTH MATERIALIZES. THE FIRST FOUR HOURS, IT FORMS AND COOLS DOWN...
NOT A HAIRBALL!
AT 4:00, THE FIRST BACTERIA APPEAR IN THE SEA...
ACHOOO!
LOT OF GERMS AROUND HERE!
AT 20:30, PLANTS MOVE INTO THE MARINE DEPTHS, FOLLOWED BY JELLYFISH...
I'M STUNNED THAT WE'D APPEAR SO LATE!
AT 22:00 PLANTS SETTLE IN ON DRY LAND, FOLLOWED BY THE FIRST INSECTS AND ANIMALS...
IN SHORT, WE GO WHERE THERE'S GRUB!
YES, I'M TALKING ABOUT YOU!
SLURP
!
DIMETRODON (IT'S A REPTILE, NOT A DINOSAUR!)
AT 22:59, THE FIRST DINOSAURS APPEAR.
YEAH!
AT 23:39, DINOSAURS DISAPPEAR AND MAMMALS DEVELOP.
TOLD YOU I WAS STRONGER THAN YOU!
HEE-HEE!
TICKTOCKTICKTOCKTICKTOCKTICKTOCK
TICKTOCKTOCKTIC
AT 23:59, OUR PRIMATE ANCESTORS BEGIN EVOLVING.
AND WE MODERN HUMANS ONLY APPEAR AT 23:59 AND 56 SECONDS!
SO WHAT ARE YOU TELLING ME?!
ARE YOU GOING TO BUY THIS WATCH FROM ME OR WHAT?
IT ISN'T EVEN 05:00 YET!
Cuckoo Clock Shoppe

ALBERTOSAURUS

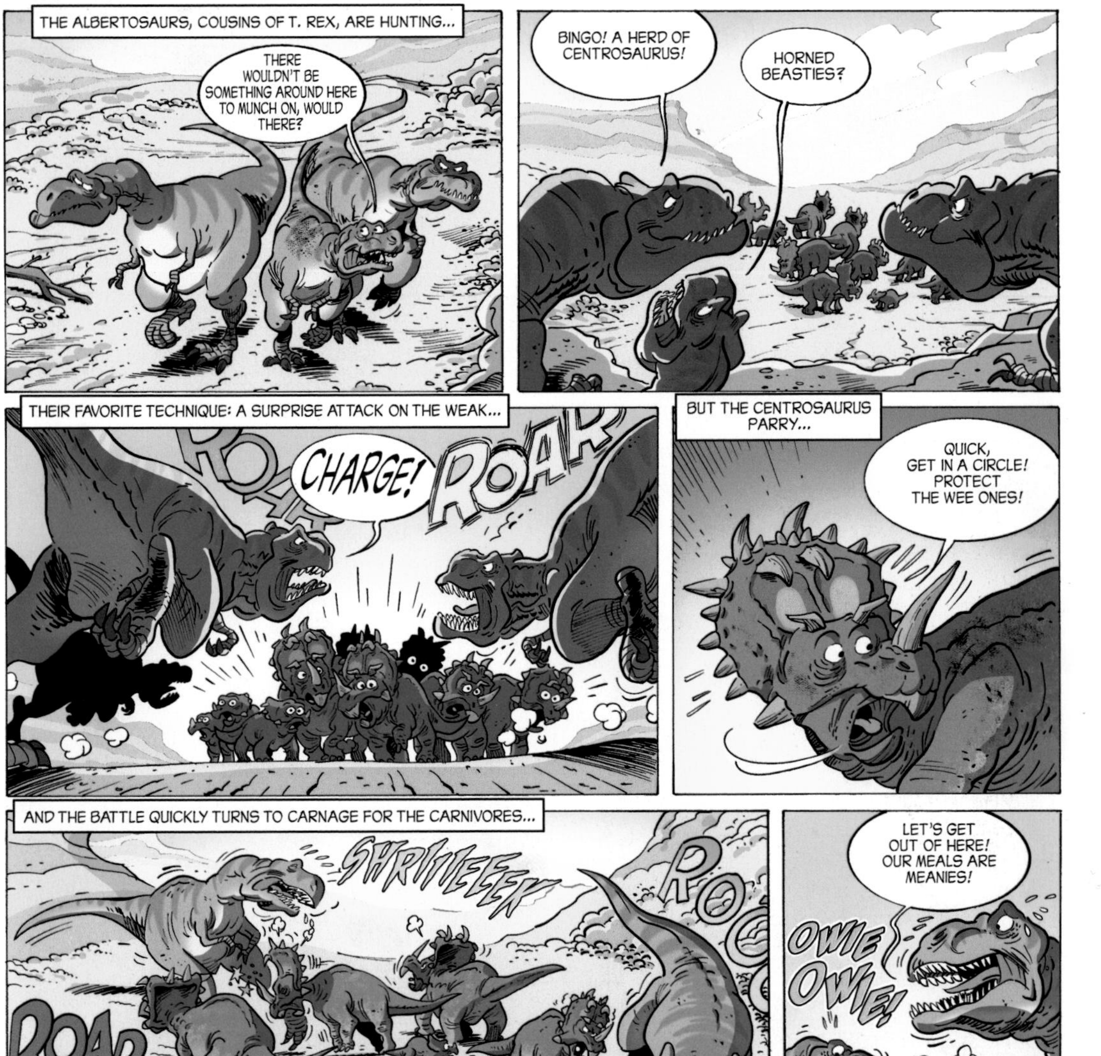
THE ALBERTOSAURS, COUSINS OF T. REX, ARE HUNTING...
THERE WOULDN'T BE SOMETHING AROUND HERE TO MUNCH ON, WOULD THERE?
BINGO! A HERD OF CENTROSAURUS!
HORNED BEASTIES?
THEIR FAVORITE TECHNIQUE: A SURPRISE ATTACK ON THE WEAK...
ROAR
CHARGE!
ROAR
BUT THE CENTROSAURUS PARRY...
QUICK, GET IN A CIRCLE! PROTECT THE WEE ONES!
AND THE BATTLE QUICKLY TURNS TO CARNAGE FOR THE CARNIVORES...
SHRIIIEEEK
ROAR
RO
LET'S GET OUT OF HERE! OUR MEALS ARE MEANIES!
OWIE OWIE!

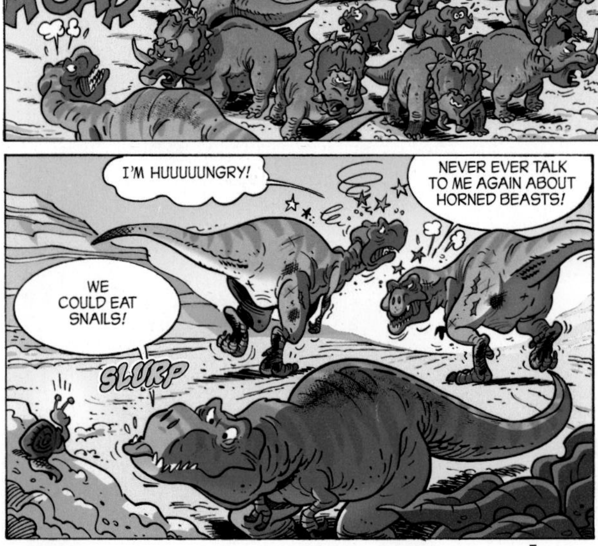
I'M HUUUUUNGRY!
NEVER EVER TALK TO ME AGAIN ABOUT HORNED BEASTS!
WE COULD EAT SNAILS!
SLURP

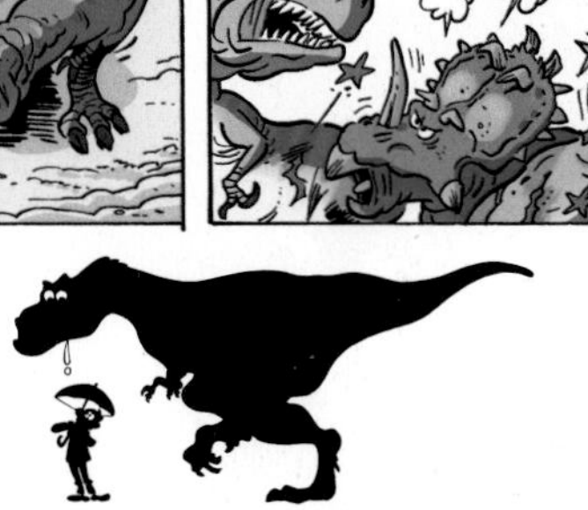

ALBERTOSAURUS

MEANING: ALBERTA (CANADIAN PROVINCE) LIZARD
PERIOD: LATE CRETACEOUS (70 MILLION YEARS AGO)
ORDER/ FAMILY: SAURISCHIA/ TYRANNOSAURIDAE
SIZE: 30 FEET LONG
WEIGHT: 6,000 LBS.
DIET: CARNIVORE
FOUND: NORTH AMERICA

PLUMERI + BLOZ

THE PROFESSION OF PALEONTOLOGY

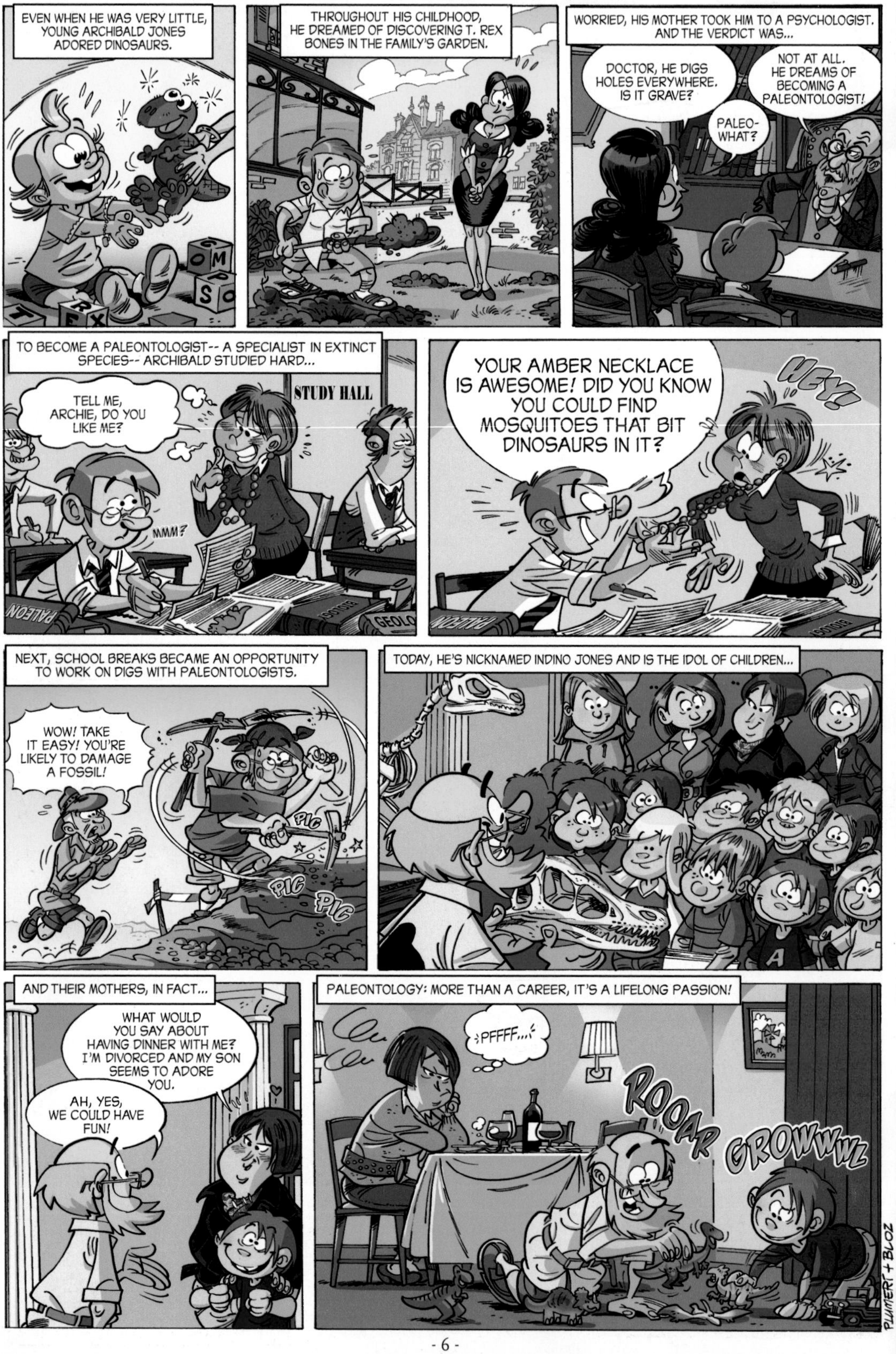
EVEN WHEN HE WAS VERY LITTLE, YOUNG ARCHIBALD JONES ADORED DINOSAURS.
THROUGHOUT HIS CHILDHOOD, HE DREAMED OF DISCOVERING T. REX BONES IN THE FAMILY'S GARDEN.
WORRIED, HIS MOTHER TOOK HIM TO A PSYCHOLOGIST. AND THE VERDICT WAS...
DOCTOR, HE DIGS HOLES EVERYWHERE. IS IT GRAVE?
NOT AT ALL. HE DREAMS OF BECOMING A PALEONTOLOGIST!
PALEO-WHAT?
TO BECOME A PALEONTOLOGIST-- A SPECIALIST IN EXTINCT SPECIES-- ARCHIBALD STUDIED HARD...
STUDY HALL
TELL ME, ARCHIE, DO YOU LIKE ME?
MMM?
YOUR AMBER NECKLACE IS AWESOME! DID YOU KNOW YOU COULD FIND MOSQUITOES THAT BIT DINOSAURS IN IT?
HEY!
NEXT, SCHOOL BREAKS BECAME AN OPPORTUNITY TO WORK ON DIGS WITH PALEONTOLOGISTS.
WOW! TAKE IT EASY! YOU'RE LIKELY TO DAMAGE A FOSSIL!
PIC
PIC
PIC
TODAY, HE'S NICKNAMED INDINO JONES AND IS THE IDOL OF CHILDREN...
AND THEIR MOTHERS, IN FACT...
WHAT WOULD YOU SAY ABOUT HAVING DINNER WITH ME? I'M DIVORCED AND MY SON SEEMS TO ADORE YOU.
AH, YES, WE COULD HAVE FUN!
PALEONTOLOGY: MORE THAN A CAREER, IT'S A LIFELONG PASSION!
PFFFF...
ROOAR
GROWWWL
PLUMERI + BLOZ

T. REX'S APPETITE

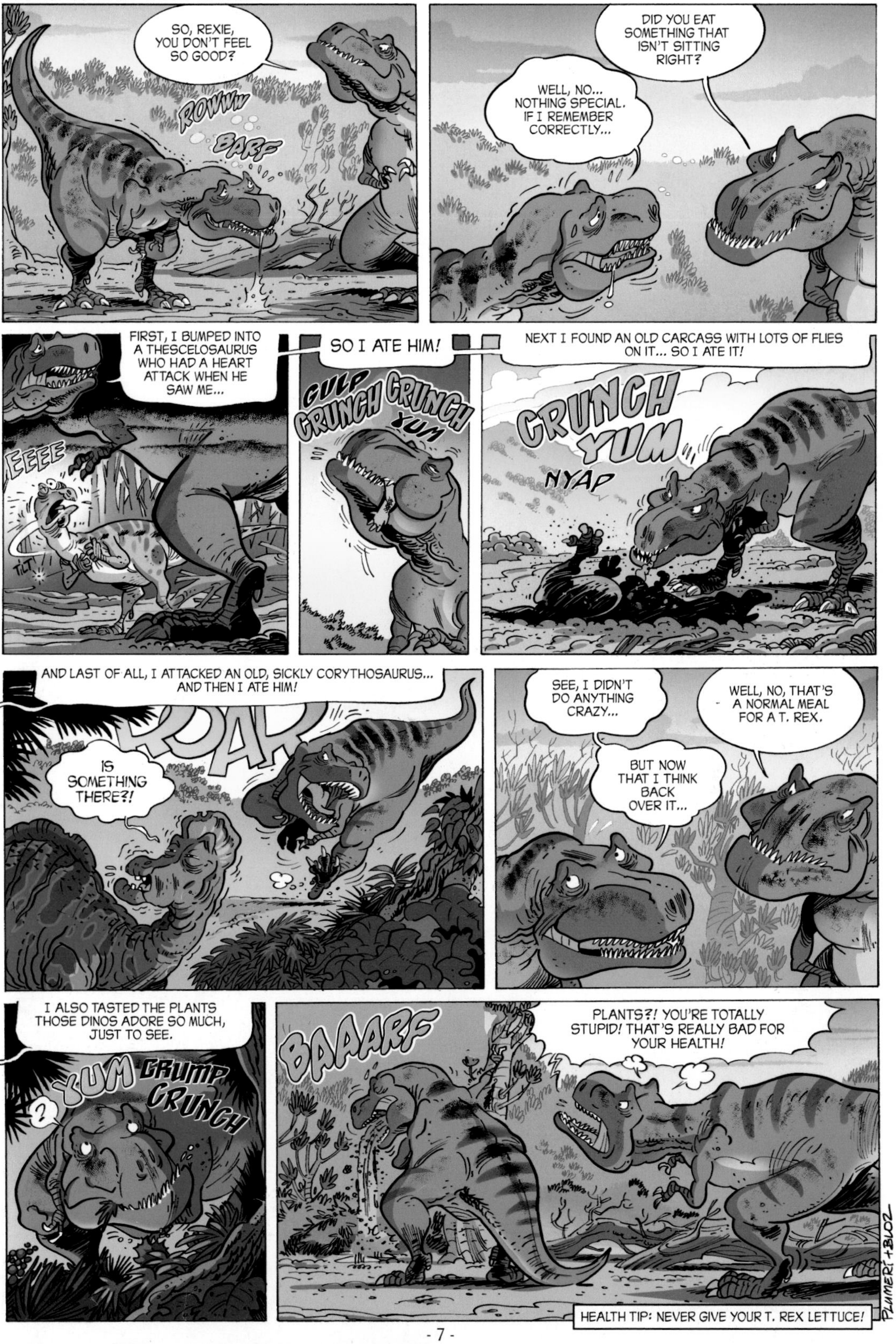

SO, REXIE, YOU DON'T FEEL SO GOOD?
ROWW
BARF
DID YOU EAT SOMETHING THAT ISN'T SITTING RIGHT?
WELL, NO... NOTHING SPECIAL. IF I REMEMBER CORRECTLY...
FIRST, I BUMPED INTO A THESCELOSAURUS WHO HAD A HEART ATTACK WHEN HE SAW ME...
EEEE
TILT
SO I ATE HIM!
GULP CRUNCH CRUNCH YUM
NEXT I FOUND AN OLD CARCASS WITH LOTS OF FLIES ON IT... SO I ATE IT!
CRUNCH YUM
NYAP
AND LAST OF ALL, I ATTACKED AN OLD, SICKLY CORYTHOSAURUS... AND THEN I ATE HIM!
ROAR
IS SOMETHING THERE?!
SEE, I DIDN'T DO ANYTHING CRAZY...
WELL, NO, THAT'S A NORMAL MEAL FOR A T. REX.
BUT NOW THAT I THINK BACK OVER IT...
I ALSO TASTED THE PLANTS THOSE DINOS ADORE SO MUCH, JUST TO SEE.
YUM CRUMP CRUNCH
?
BAAARF
PLANTS?! YOU'RE TOTALLY STUPID! THAT'S REALLY BAD FOR YOUR HEALTH!
HEALTH TIP: NEVER GIVE YOUR T. REX LETTUCE!
PLUMERI + BLOZ

THE SIZE OF DINOSAURS

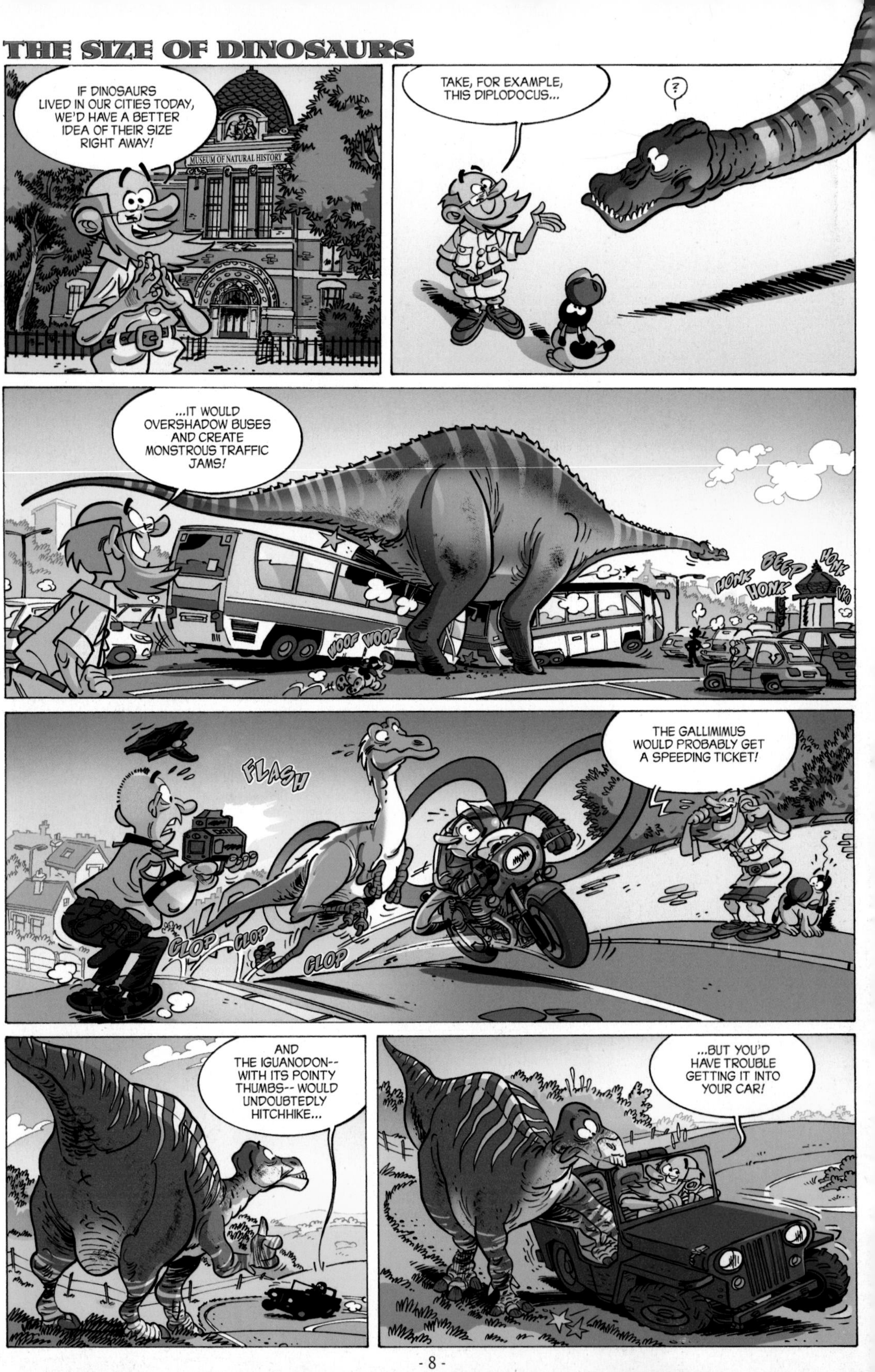

IF DINOSAURS LIVED IN OUR CITIES TODAY, WE'D HAVE A BETTER IDEA OF THEIR SIZE RIGHT AWAY!
MUSEUM OF NATURAL HISTORY
TAKE, FOR EXAMPLE, THIS DIPLODOCUS...
?
...IT WOULD OVERSHADOW BUSES AND CREATE MONSTROUS TRAFFIC JAMS!
WOOF WOOF
HONK
BEEP
HONK
HONK
FLASH
CLOP
CLOP
CLOP
THE GALLIMIMUS WOULD PROBABLY GET A SPEEDING TICKET!
AND THE IGUANODON-- WITH ITS POINTY THUMBS-- WOULD UNDOUBTEDLY HITCHHIKE...
...BUT YOU'D HAVE TROUBLE GETTING IT INTO YOUR CAR!

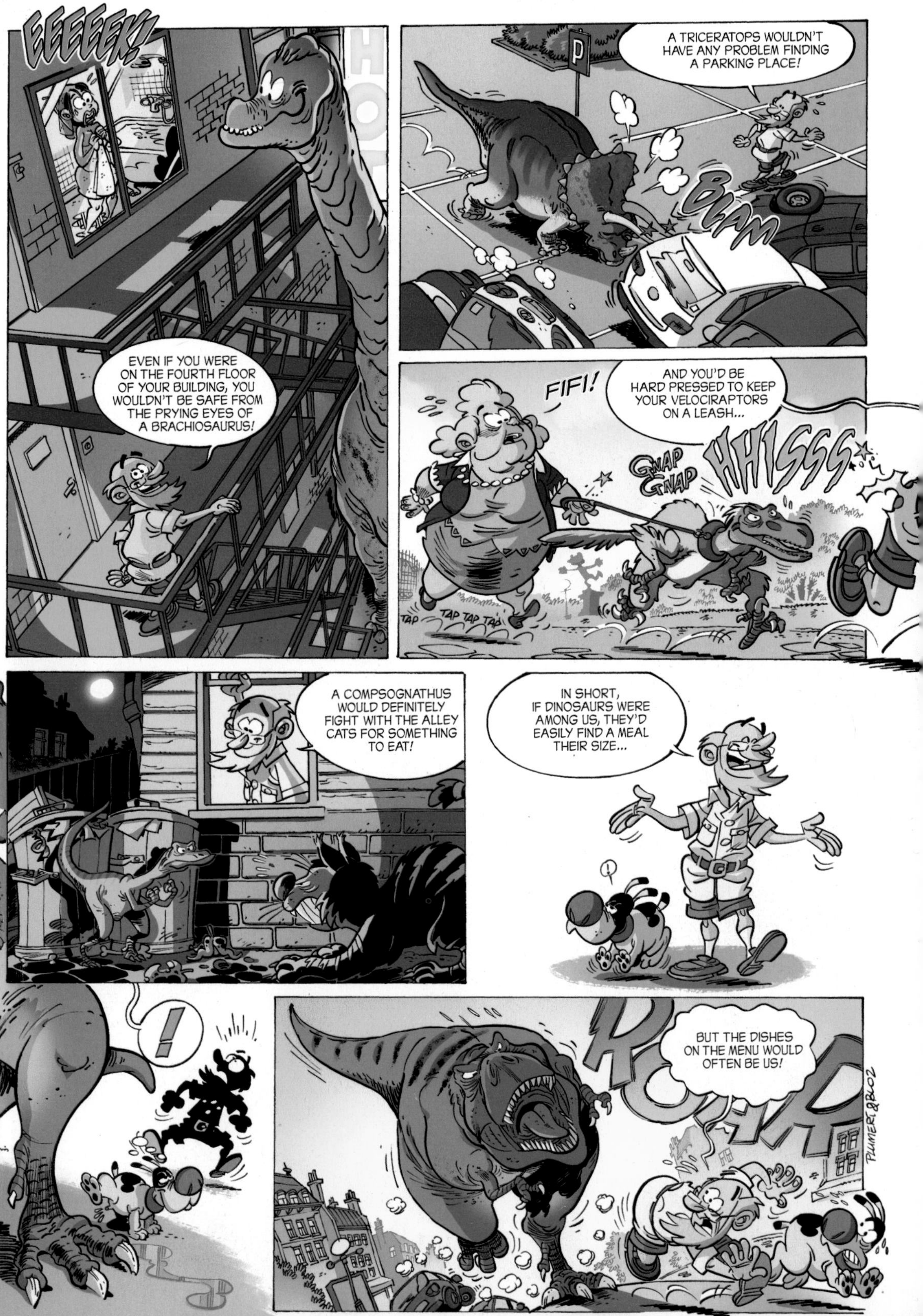
EEEEEK!
EVEN IF YOU WERE ON THE FOURTH FLOOR OF YOUR BUILDING, YOU WOULDN'T BE SAFE FROM THE PRYING EYES OF A BRACHIOSAURUS!
P
A TRICERATOPS WOULDN'T HAVE ANY PROBLEM FINDING A PARKING PLACE!
BLAM
FIFI!
AND YOU'D BE HARD PRESSED TO KEEP YOUR VELOCIRAPTORS ON A LEASH...
GNAP GNAP
HHISSS
TAP TAP TAP TAP
A COMPSOGNATHUS WOULD DEFINITELY FIGHT WITH THE ALLEY CATS FOR SOMETHING TO EAT!
IN SHORT, IF DINOSAURS WERE AMONG US, THEY'D EASILY FIND A MEAL THEIR SIZE...
!
!
BUT THE DISHES ON THE MENU WOULD OFTEN BE US!
PLUMERI & BLOZ

DINOSAUR FEET

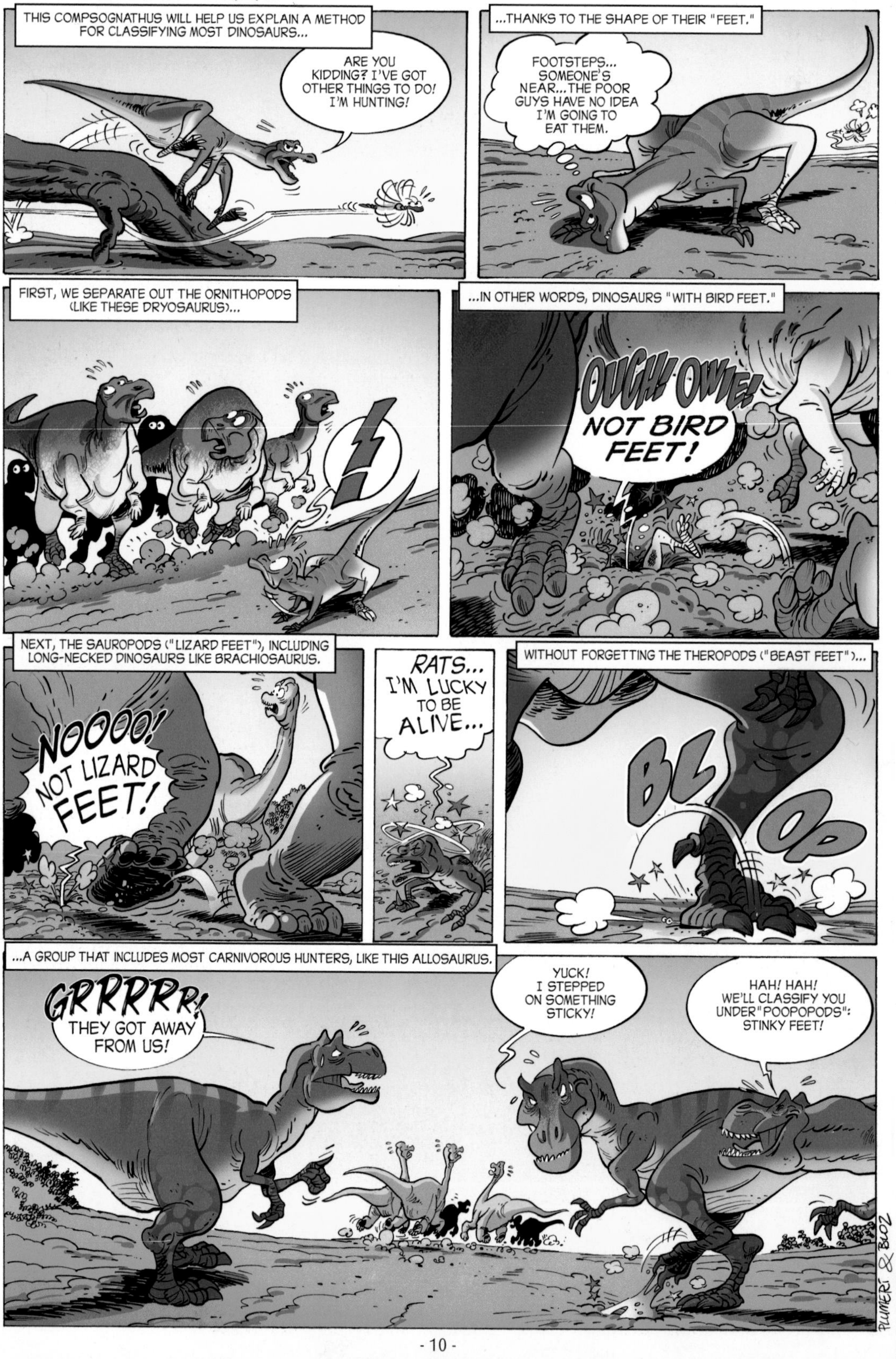

THIS COMPSOGNATHUS WILL HELP US EXPLAIN A METHOD FOR CLASSIFYING MOST DINOSAURS...
ARE YOU KIDDING? I'VE GOT OTHER THINGS TO DO! I'M HUNTING!
...THANKS TO THE SHAPE OF THEIR "FEET."
FOOTSTEPS... SOMEONE'S NEAR...THE POOR GUYS HAVE NO IDEA I'M GOING TO EAT THEM.
FIRST, WE SEPARATE OUT THE ORNITHOPODS (LIKE THESE DRYOSAURUS)...
...IN OTHER WORDS, DINOSAURS "WITH BIRD FEET."
OUCH! OWIE! NOT BIRD FEET!
NEXT, THE SAUROPODS ("LIZARD FEET"), INCLUDING LONG-NECKED DINOSAURS LIKE BRACHIOSAURUS.
NOOOO! NOT LIZARD FEET!
RATS... I'M LUCKY TO BE ALIVE...
WITHOUT FORGETTING THE THEROPODS ("BEAST FEET")...
BLOOP
...A GROUP THAT INCLUDES MOST CARNIVOROUS HUNTERS, LIKE THIS ALLOSAURUS.
GRRRRR! THEY GOT AWAY FROM US!
YUCK! I STEPPED ON SOMETHING STICKY!
HAH! HAH! WE'LL CLASSIFY YOU UNDER "POOPOPODS": STINKY FEET!
PLUMERI & BLOZ

EUOPLOCEPHALUS

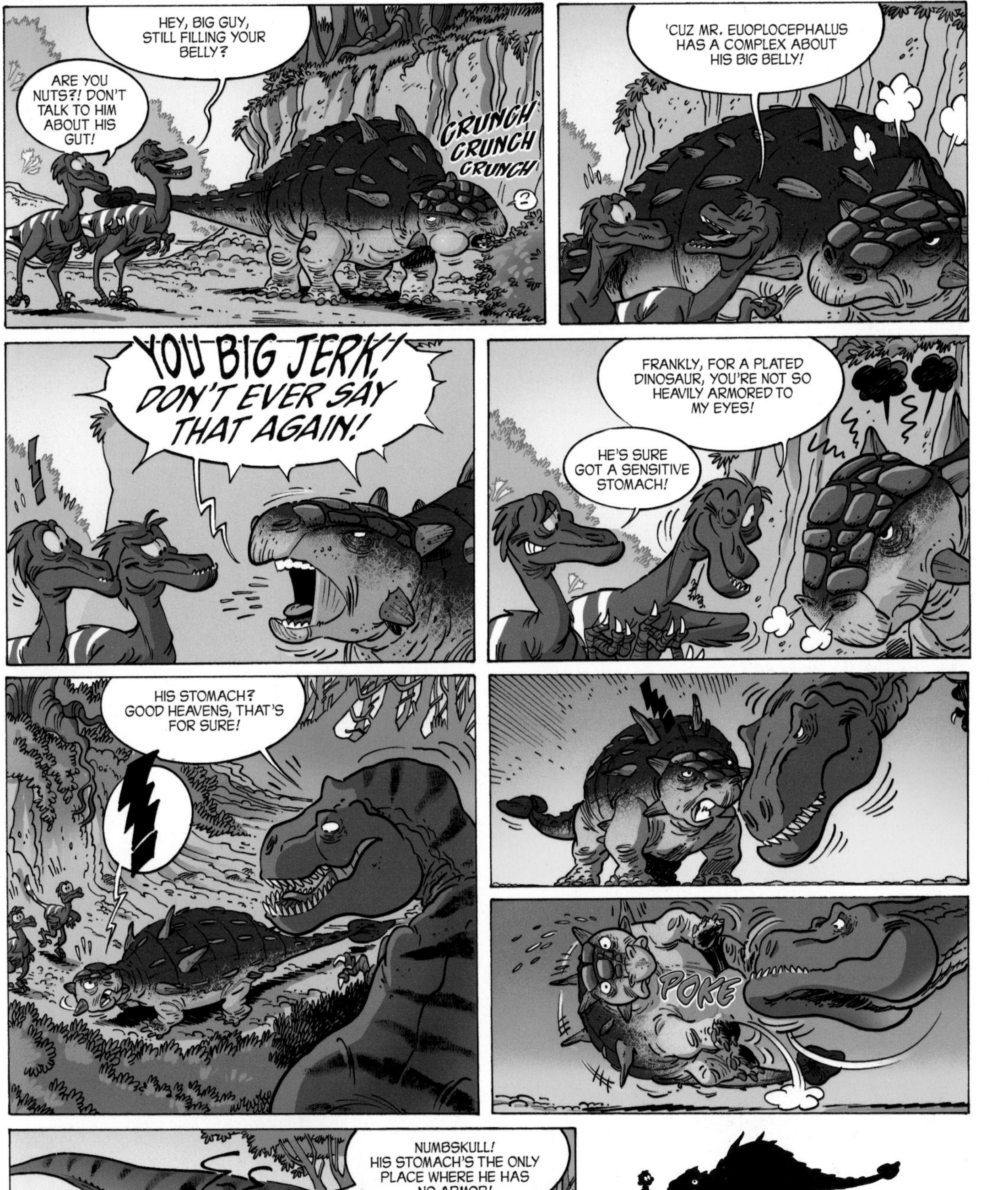
HEY, BIG GUY, STILL FILLING YOUR BELLY?
ARE YOU NUTS?! DON'T TALK TO HIM ABOUT HIS GUT!
CRUNCH CRUNCH CRUNCH
?
'CUZ MR. EUOPLOCEPHALUS HAS A COMPLEX ABOUT HIS BIG BELLY!
YOU BIG JERK! DON'T EVER SAY THAT AGAIN!
FRANKLY, FOR A PLATED DINOSAUR, YOU'RE NOT SO HEAVILY ARMORED TO MY EYES!
HE'S SURE GOT A SENSITIVE STOMACH!
HIS STOMACH? GOOD HEAVENS, THAT'S FOR SURE!
POKE

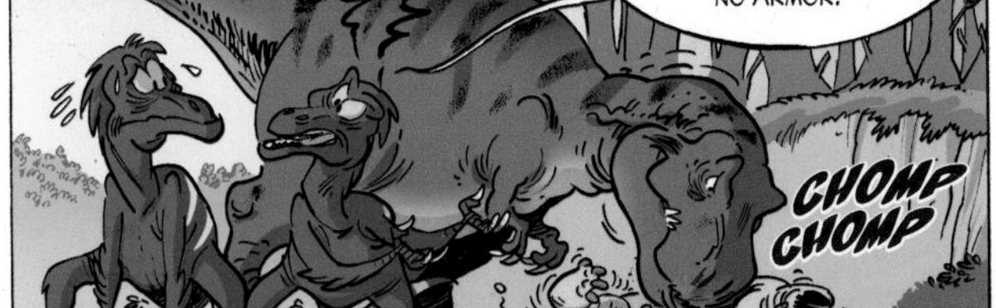
NUMBSKULL! HIS STOMACH'S THE ONLY PLACE WHERE HE HAS NO ARMOR!
CHOMP CHOMP

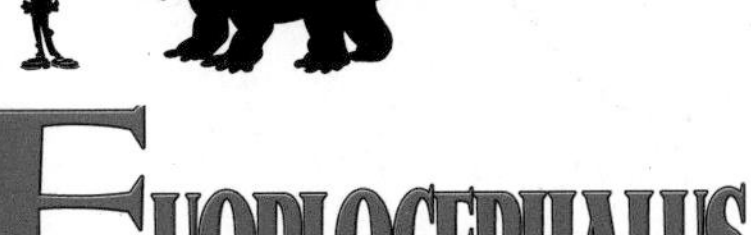

EUOPLOCEPHALUS

MEANING: WELL-ARMED HEAD
PERIOD: LATE CRETACEOUS (80-66 MILLION YEARS AGO)
ORDER/ FAMILY: ORNITHISCHIA/ ANKYLOSAURIDAE
SIZE: 20 FEET LONG
WEIGHT: 4,400 POUNDS
DIET: HERBIVORE
FOUND: NORTH AMERICA

PLUMERI & BLOZ

CARNOTAURUS

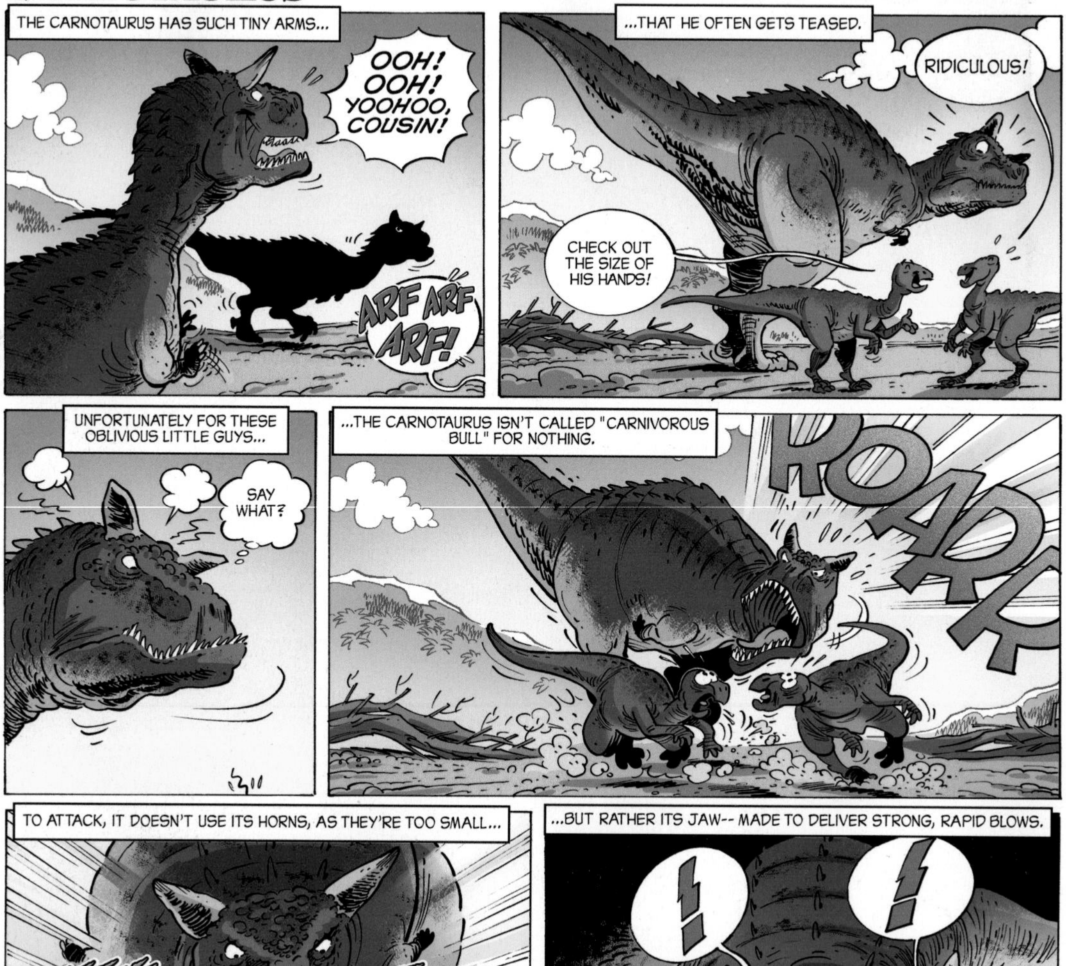
THE CARNOTAURUS HAS SUCH TINY ARMS...
OOH! OOH! YOOHOO, COUSIN!
ARF ARF ARF!
...THAT HE OFTEN GETS TEASED.
RIDICULOUS!
CHECK OUT THE SIZE OF HIS HANDS!
UNFORTUNATELY FOR THESE OBLIVIOUS LITTLE GUYS...
SAY WHAT?
...THE CARNOTAURUS ISN'T CALLED "CARNIVOROUS BULL" FOR NOTHING.
ROARR
TO ATTACK, IT DOESN'T USE ITS HORNS, AS THEY'RE TOO SMALL...
EEEEEK!
EEERK!
...BUT RATHER ITS JAW-- MADE TO DELIVER STRONG, RAPID BLOWS.
!
!
OUCH!
OW!
OUCH!
OWIE!

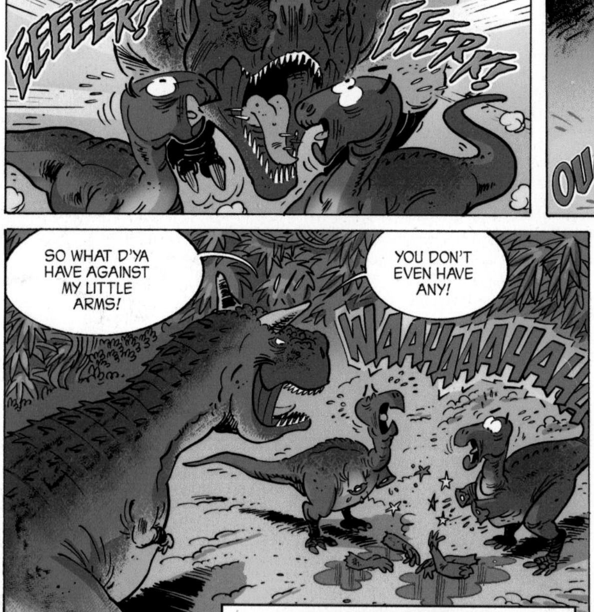
SO WHAT D'YA HAVE AGAINST MY LITTLE ARMS!
YOU DON'T EVEN HAVE ANY!
WAAAAAAAH
IN SUM, NEVER MAKE FUN OF A CARNOTAURUS!

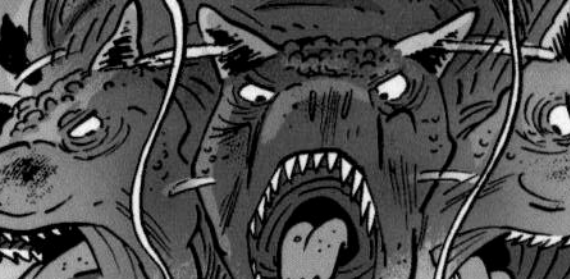

CARNOTAURUS

MEANING: CARNIVOROUS BULL
PERIOD: LATE CRETACEOUS (83.5-65.5 MILLION YEARS AGO)
ORDER/ FAMILY: SAURISCHIA/ ABELISAURIDAE
SIZE: 26 FEET LONG
WEIGHT: 3,300 POUNDS
DIET: CARNIVORE
FOUND: SOUTH AMERICA

PLUMERI+BLOZ

T. REX'S BITE

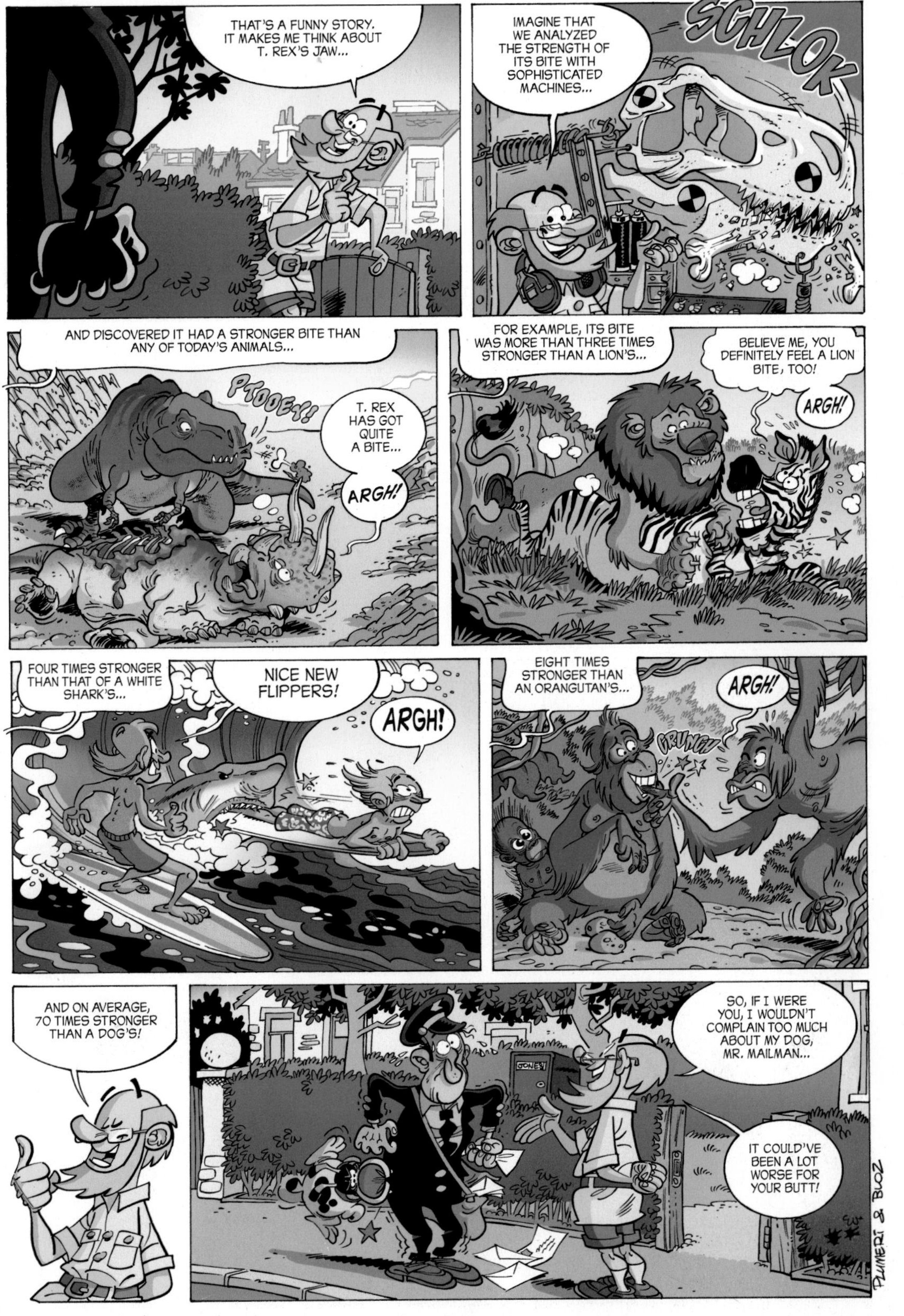

THAT'S A FUNNY STORY. IT MAKES ME THINK ABOUT T. REX'S JAW...
IMAGINE THAT WE ANALYZED THE STRENGTH OF ITS BITE WITH SOPHISTICATED MACHINES...
SCHLOK
AND DISCOVERED IT HAD A STRONGER BITE THAN ANY OF TODAY'S ANIMALS...
PTOOEY!
T. REX HAS GOT QUITE A BITE...
ARGH!
FOR EXAMPLE, ITS BITE WAS MORE THAN THREE TIMES STRONGER THAN A LION'S...
BELIEVE ME, YOU DEFINITELY FEEL A LION BITE, TOO!
ARGH!
FOUR TIMES STRONGER THAN THAT OF A WHITE SHARK'S...
NICE NEW FLIPPERS!
ARGH!
EIGHT TIMES STRONGER THAN AN ORANGUTAN'S...
ARGH!
CRUNCH
AND ON AVERAGE, 70 TIMES STRONGER THAN A DOG'S!
SO, IF I WERE YOU, I WOULDN'T COMPLAIN TOO MUCH ABOUT MY DOG, MR. MAILMAN...
JONES
IT COULD'VE BEEN A LOT WORSE FOR YOUR BUTT!
PLUMERI & BLOZ

FALSE IDEAS ABOUT DINOSAURS

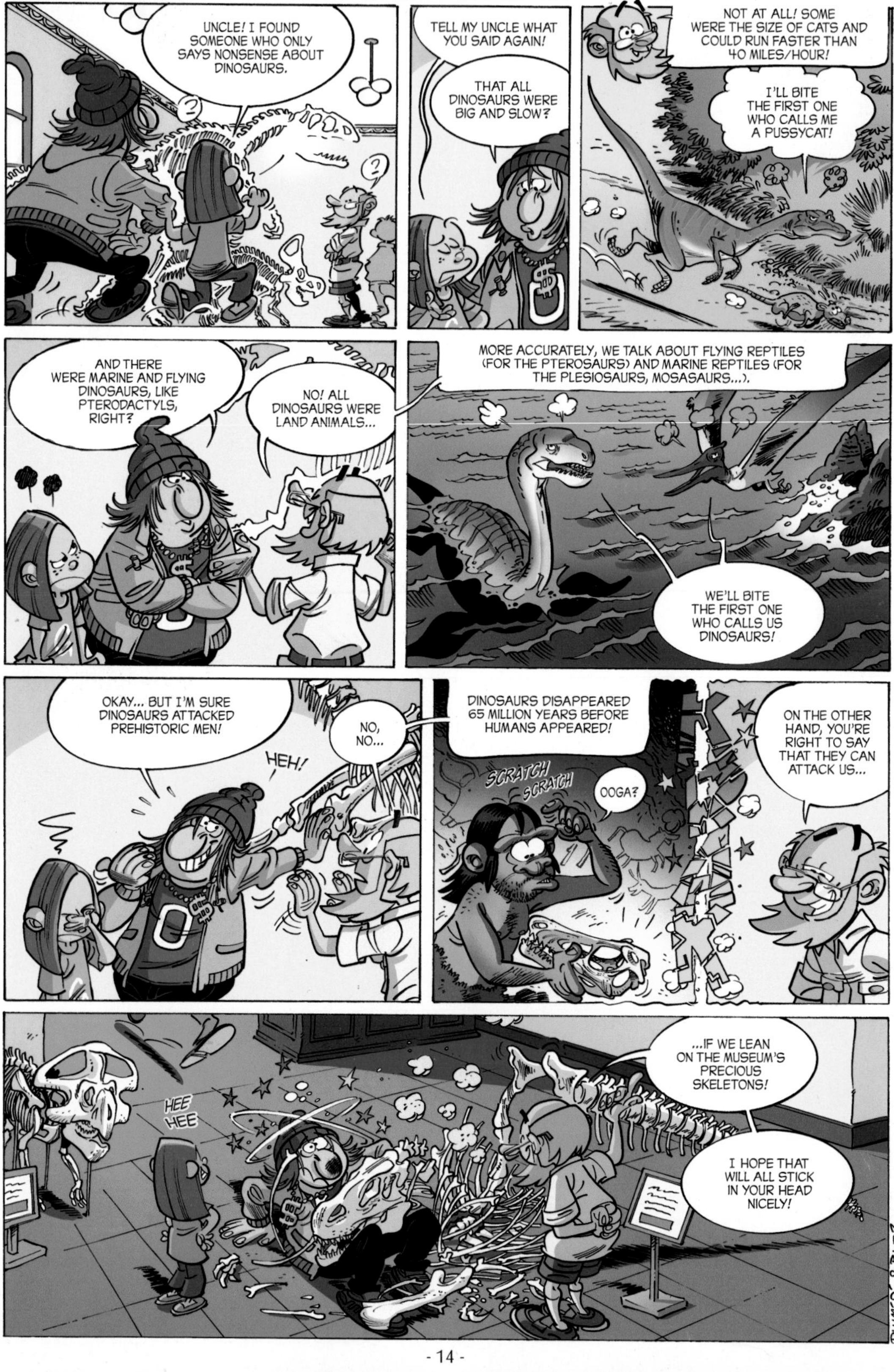

UNCLE! I FOUND SOMEONE WHO ONLY SAYS NONSENSE ABOUT DINOSAURS.
?
?
TELL MY UNCLE WHAT YOU SAID AGAIN!
THAT ALL DINOSAURS WERE BIG AND SLOW?
NOT AT ALL! SOME WERE THE SIZE OF CATS AND COULD RUN FASTER THAN 40 MILES/HOUR!
I'LL BITE THE FIRST ONE WHO CALLS ME A PUSSYCAT!
AND THERE WERE MARINE AND FLYING DINOSAURS, LIKE PTERODACTYLS, RIGHT?
NO! ALL DINOSAURS WERE LAND ANIMALS...
MORE ACCURATELY, WE TALK ABOUT FLYING REPTILES (FOR THE PTEROSAURS) AND MARINE REPTILES (FOR THE PLESIOSAURS, MOSASAURS...).
WE'LL BITE THE FIRST ONE WHO CALLS US DINOSAURS!
OKAY... BUT I'M SURE DINOSAURS ATTACKED PREHISTORIC MEN!
NO, NO...
HEH!
DINOSAURS DISAPPEARED 65 MILLION YEARS BEFORE HUMANS APPEARED!
SCRATCH
SCRATCH
OOGA?
ON THE OTHER HAND, YOU'RE RIGHT TO SAY THAT THEY CAN ATTACK US...
HEE HEE
...IF WE LEAN ON THE MUSEUM'S PRECIOUS SKELETONS!
I HOPE THAT WILL ALL STICK IN YOUR HEAD NICELY!
PLUMERI & BLOZ

REPRODUCTION

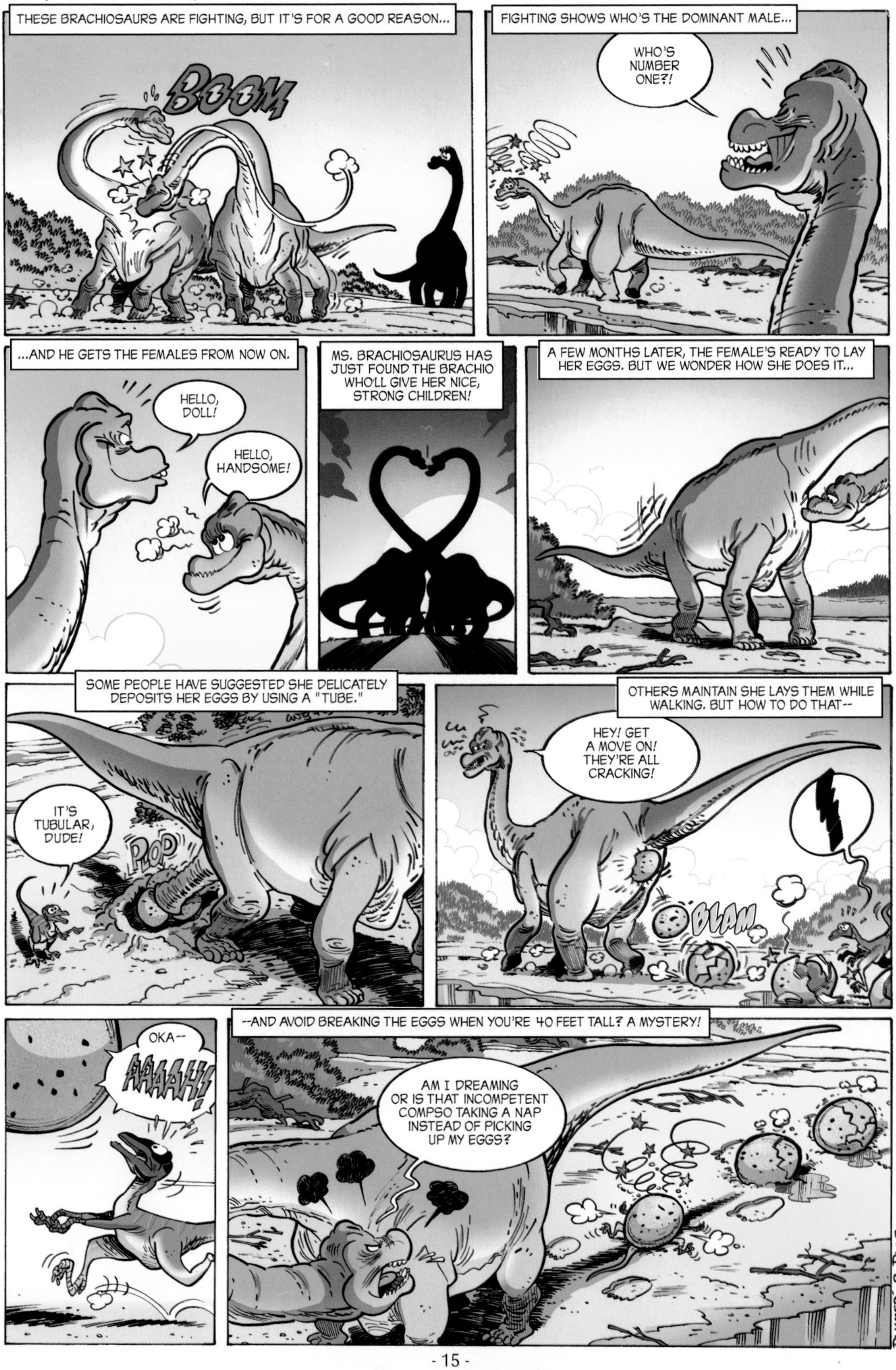

THESE BRACHIOSAURS ARE FIGHTING, BUT IT'S FOR A GOOD REASON...
BOOM
FIGHTING SHOWS WHO'S THE DOMINANT MALE...
WHO'S NUMBER ONE?!
...AND HE GETS THE FEMALES FROM NOW ON.
HELLO, DOLL!
HELLO, HANDSOME!
MS. BRACHIOSAURUS HAS JUST FOUND THE BRACHIO WHO'LL GIVE HER NICE, STRONG CHILDREN!
A FEW MONTHS LATER, THE FEMALE'S READY TO LAY HER EGGS. BUT WE WONDER HOW SHE DOES IT...
SOME PEOPLE HAVE SUGGESTED SHE DELICATELY DEPOSITS HER EGGS BY USING A "TUBE."
IT'S TUBULAR, DUDE!
PLOP
OTHERS MAINTAIN SHE LAYS THEM WHILE WALKING. BUT HOW TO DO THAT--
HEY! GET A MOVE ON! THEY'RE ALL CRACKING!
BLAM
OKA--
AAAAH!
--AND AVOID BREAKING THE EGGS WHEN YOU'RE 40 FEET TALL? A MYSTERY!
AM I DREAMING OR IS THAT INCOMPETENT COMPSO TAKING A NAP INSTEAD OF PICKING UP MY EGGS?
PLUMERI & BLOZ

T. REX: PREDATOR OR SCAVENGER?

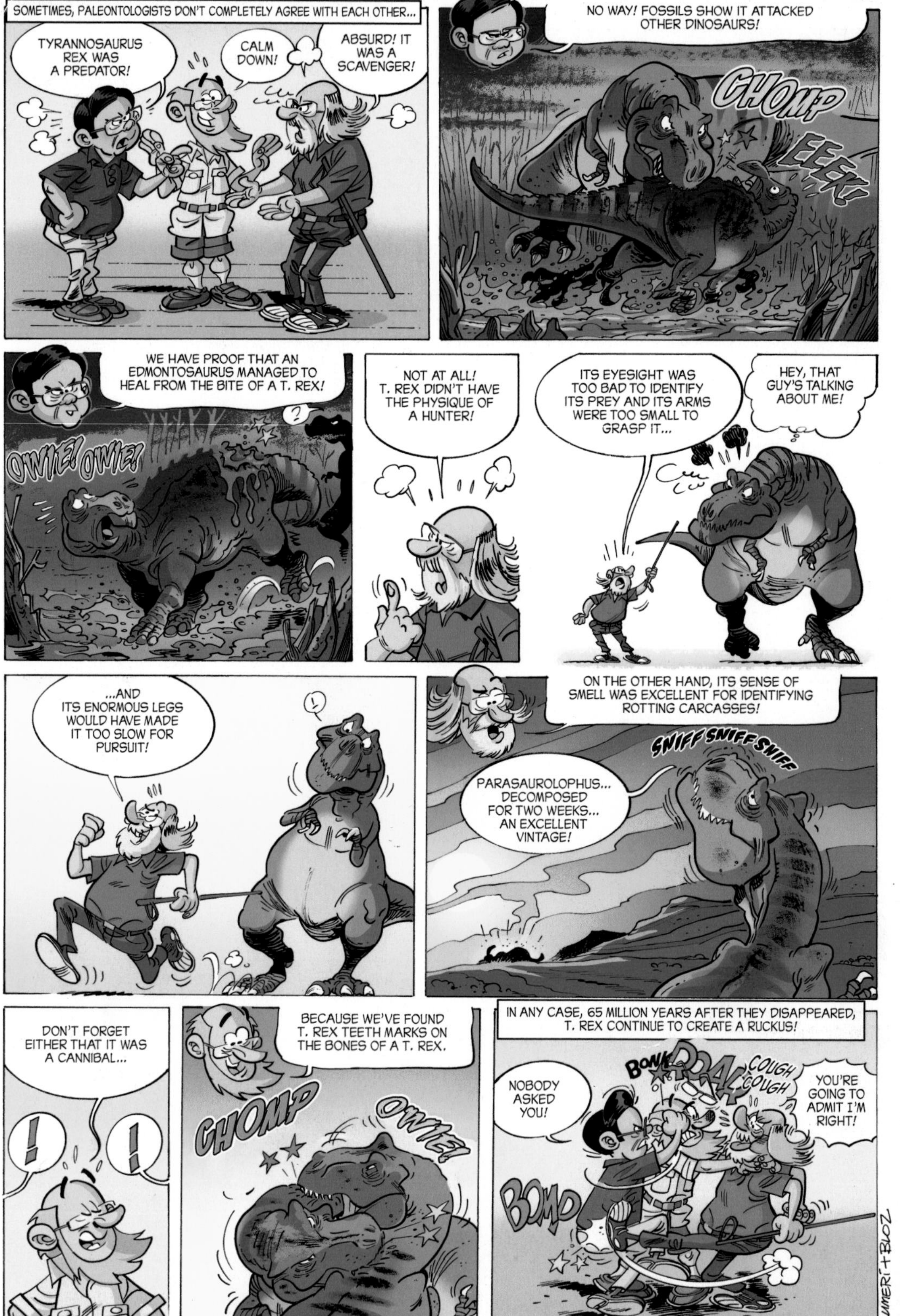

SOMETIMES, PALEONTOLOGISTS DON'T COMPLETELY AGREE WITH EACH OTHER...
TYRANNOSAURUS REX WAS A PREDATOR!
CALM DOWN!
ABSURD! IT WAS A SCAVENGER!
NO WAY! FOSSILS SHOW IT ATTACKED OTHER DINOSAURS!
CHOMP
EEEK!
WE HAVE PROOF THAT AN EDMONTOSAURUS MANAGED TO HEAL FROM THE BITE OF A T. REX!
OWIE! OWIE!
?
NOT AT ALL! T. REX DIDN'T HAVE THE PHYSIQUE OF A HUNTER!
ITS EYESIGHT WAS TOO BAD TO IDENTIFY ITS PREY AND ITS ARMS WERE TOO SMALL TO GRASP IT...
HEY, THAT GUY'S TALKING ABOUT ME!
...AND ITS ENORMOUS LEGS WOULD HAVE MADE IT TOO SLOW FOR PURSUIT!
!
ON THE OTHER HAND, ITS SENSE OF SMELL WAS EXCELLENT FOR IDENTIFYING ROTTING CARCASSES!
SNIFF SNIFF SNIFF
PARASAUROLOPHUS... DECOMPOSED FOR TWO WEEKS... AN EXCELLENT VINTAGE!
DON'T FORGET EITHER THAT IT WAS A CANNIBAL...
!
!
BECAUSE WE'VE FOUND T. REX TEETH MARKS ON THE BONES OF A T. REX.
CHOMP
OWIE!
IN ANY CASE, 65 MILLION YEARS AFTER THEY DISAPPEARED, T. REX CONTINUE TO CREATE A RUCKUS!
BONK
ROAR
COUGH COUGH
NOBODY ASKED YOU!
YOU'RE GOING TO ADMIT I'M RIGHT!
BOMD
PLUMERI + BLOZ

OSTRICH-LIKE DINOSAURS

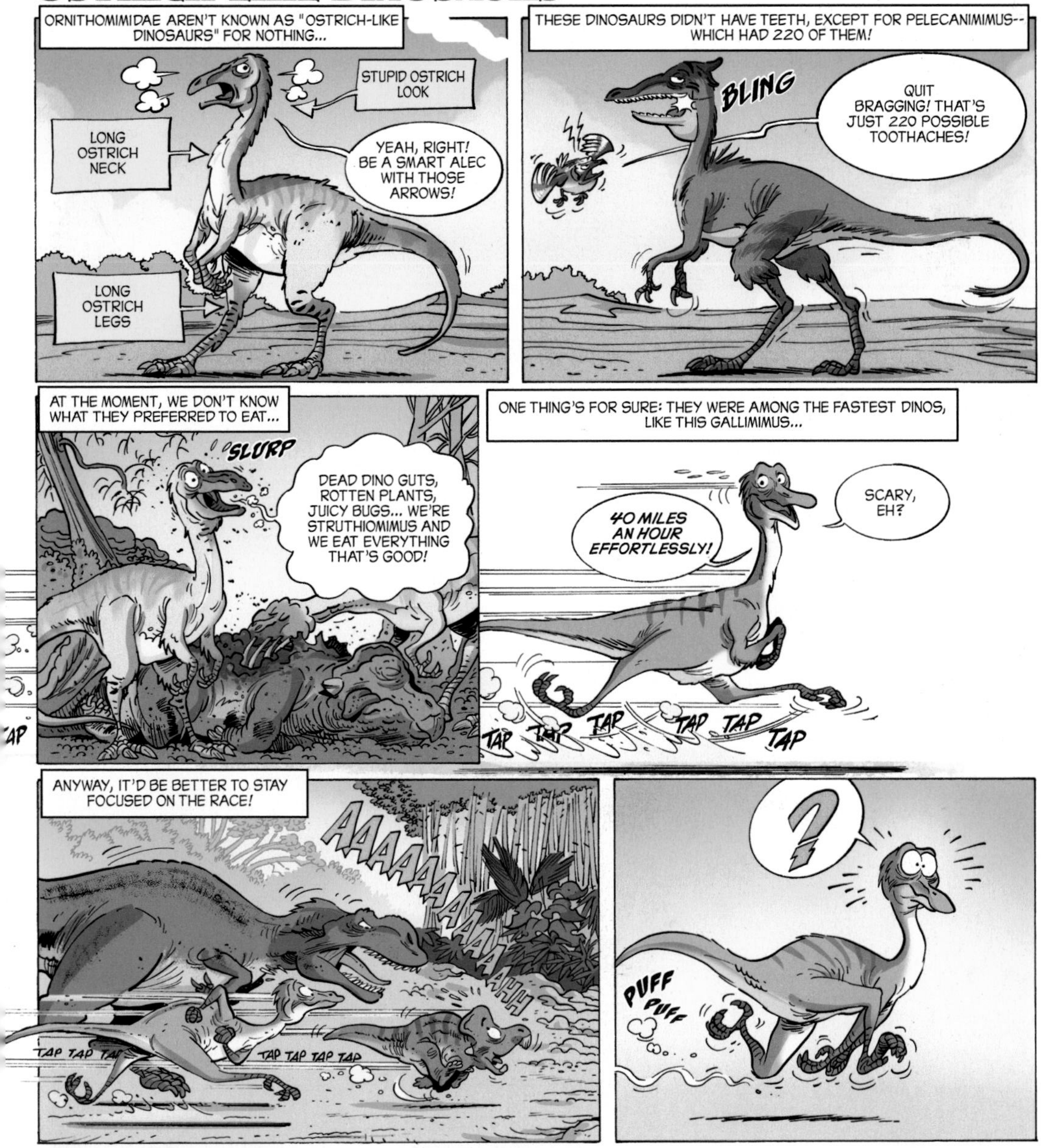
ORNITHOMIMIDAE AREN'T KNOWN AS "OSTRICH-LIKE DINOSAURS" FOR NOTHING...
STUPID OSTRICH LOOK
LONG OSTRICH NECK
YEAH, RIGHT! BE A SMART ALEC WITH THOSE ARROWS!
LONG OSTRICH LEGS
THESE DINOSAURS DIDN'T HAVE TEETH, EXCEPT FOR PELECANIMIMUS--WHICH HAD 220 OF THEM!
BLING
QUIT BRAGGING! THAT'S JUST 220 POSSIBLE TOOTHACHES!
AT THE MOMENT, WE DON'T KNOW WHAT THEY PREFERRED TO EAT...
SLURP
DEAD DINO GUTS, ROTTEN PLANTS, JUICY BUGS... WE'RE STRUTHIOMIMUS AND WE EAT EVERYTHING THAT'S GOOD!
ONE THING'S FOR SURE: THEY WERE AMONG THE FASTEST DINOS, LIKE THIS GALLIMIMUS...
40 MILES AN HOUR EFFORTLESSLY!
SCARY, EH?
TAP TAP TAP TAP TAP TAP
ANYWAY, IT'D BE BETTER TO STAY FOCUSED ON THE RACE!
AAAAAAAAAAAAAAHH
TAP TAP TAP
TAP TAP TAP TAP
?
PUFF PUFF

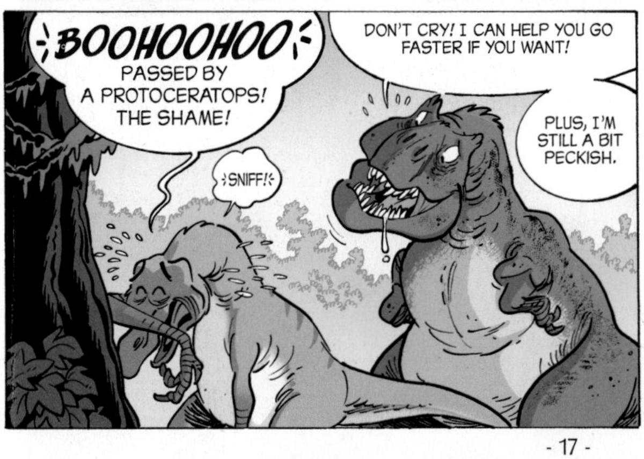
BOOHOOHOO PASSED BY A PROTOCERATOPS! THE SHAME!
SNIFF!
DON'T CRY! I CAN HELP YOU GO FASTER IF YOU WANT!
PLUS, I'M STILL A BIT PECKISH.

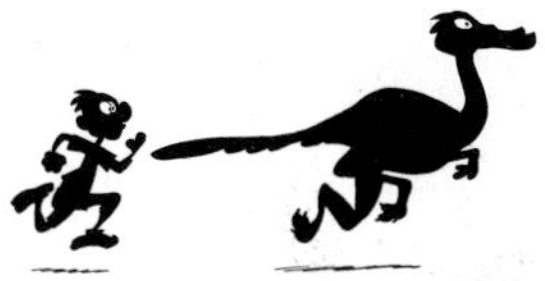

GALLIMIMUS

MEANING: CHICKEN MIMIC
PERIOD: LATE CRETACEOUS (75-70 MILLION YEARS AGO)
ORDER/ FAMILY: SAURISCHIA/ ORNITHOMIMIDAE
SIZE: 20 FEET LONG
WEIGHT: 1,100LBS.
DIET: OMNIVORE?
FOUND: MONGOLIA

PLUMERI + BLOZ

THE LITTLE DINOSAUR

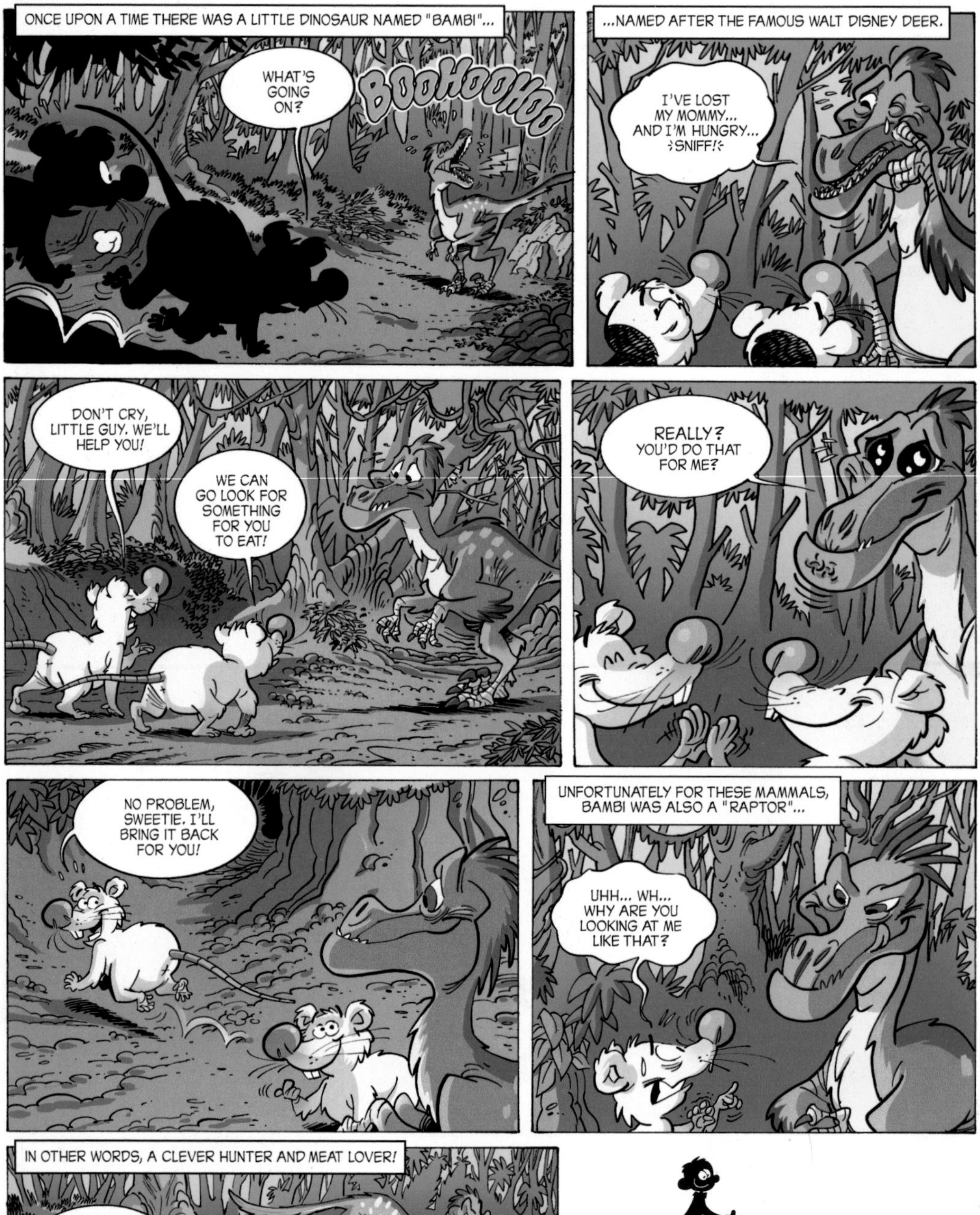
ONCE UPON A TIME THERE WAS A LITTLE DINOSAUR NAMED "BAMBI"...
WHAT'S GOING ON?
BOOHOOHOOHOO
...NAMED AFTER THE FAMOUS WALT DISNEY DEER.
I'VE LOST MY MOMMY... AND I'M HUNGRY... *SNIFF!*
DON'T CRY, LITTLE GUY. WE'LL HELP YOU!
WE CAN GO LOOK FOR SOMETHING FOR YOU TO EAT!
REALLY? YOU'D DO THAT FOR ME?
NO PROBLEM, SWEETIE. I'LL BRING IT BACK FOR YOU!
UNFORTUNATELY FOR THESE MAMMALS, BAMBI WAS ALSO A "RAPTOR"...
UHH... WH... WHY ARE YOU LOOKING AT ME LIKE THAT?

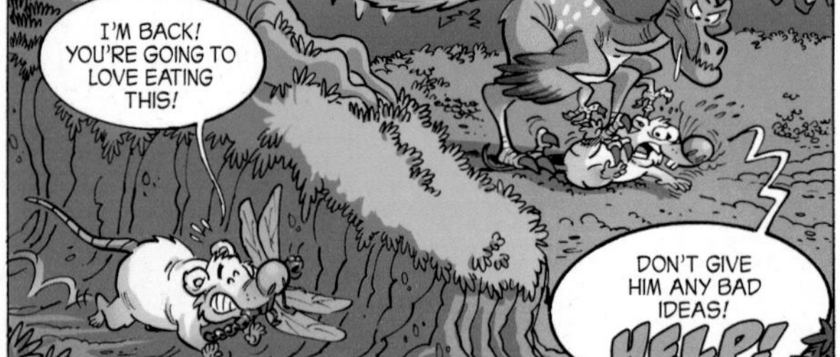
IN OTHER WORDS, A CLEVER HUNTER AND MEAT LOVER!
I'M BACK! YOU'RE GOING TO LOVE EATING THIS!
DON'T GIVE HIM ANY BAD IDEAS!
HELP!

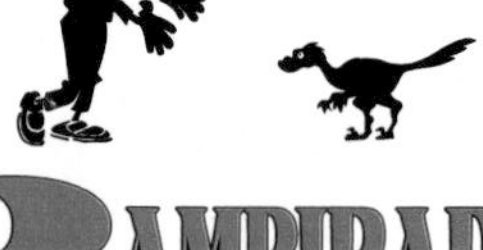

BAMBIRAPTOR

MEANING: BAMBI THIEF
PERIOD: LATE CRETACEOUS (80-72 MILLION YEARS AGO)
ORDER/ FAMILY: SAURISCHIA/ DROMAEOSAURIDAE
SIZE: 3 FEET LONG
WEIGHT: 5 LBS.
DIET: CARNIVORE
FOUND: NORTH AMERICA

PLUMERI PAN & DUMBLOZ

ALBERTOSAURUS VS CARNOTAURUS

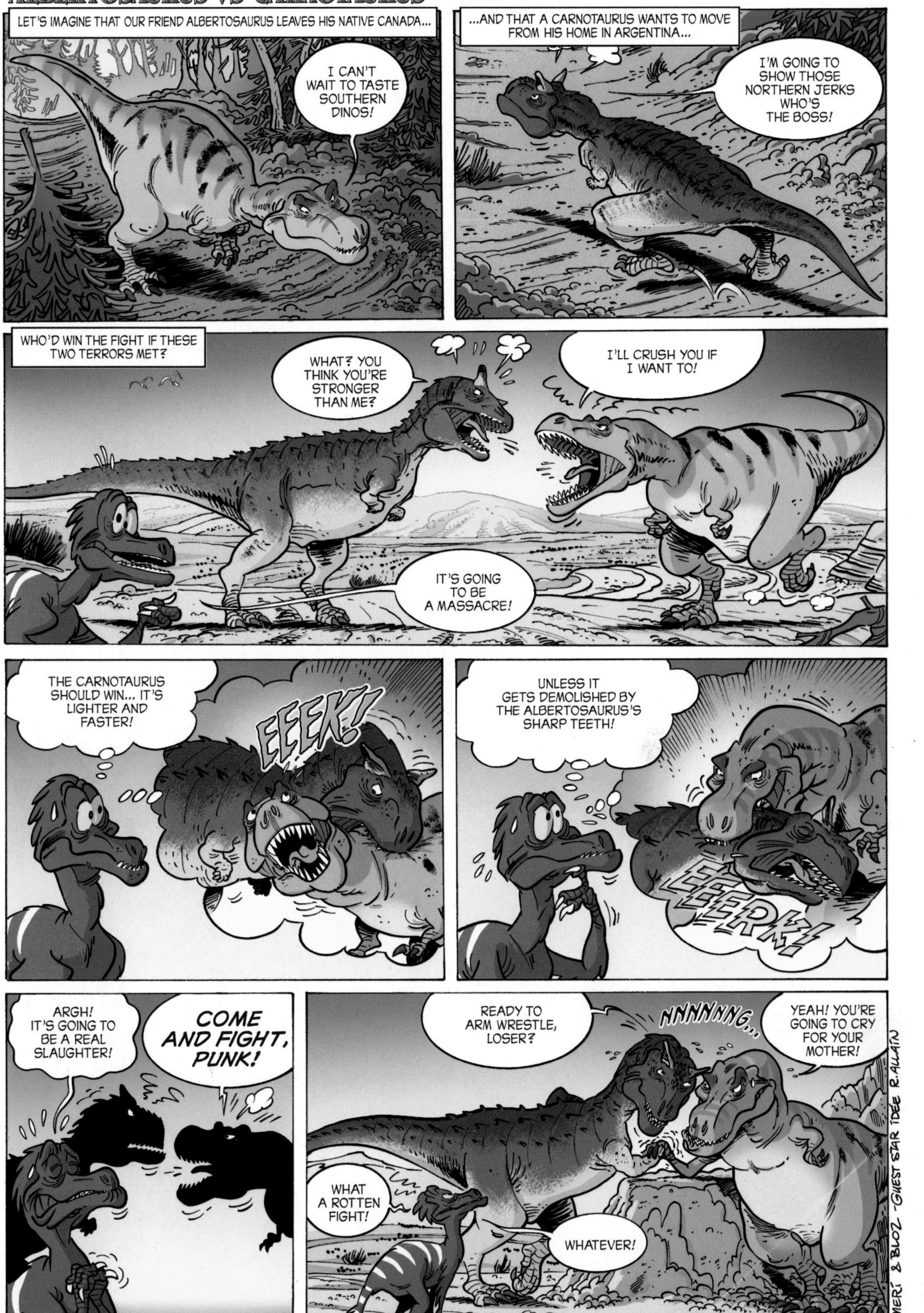

LET'S IMAGINE THAT OUR FRIEND ALBERTOSAURUS LEAVES HIS NATIVE CANADA...
I CAN'T WAIT TO TASTE SOUTHERN DINOS!
...AND THAT A CARNOTAURUS WANTS TO MOVE FROM HIS HOME IN ARGENTINA...
I'M GOING TO SHOW THOSE NORTHERN JERKS WHO'S THE BOSS!
WHO'D WIN THE FIGHT IF THESE TWO TERRORS MET?
WHAT? YOU THINK YOU'RE STRONGER THAN ME?
I'LL CRUSH YOU IF I WANT TO!
IT'S GOING TO BE A MASSACRE!
THE CARNOTAURUS SHOULD WIN... IT'S LIGHTER AND FASTER!
EEEK!!
UNLESS IT GETS DEMOLISHED BY THE ALBERTOSAURUS'S SHARP TEETH!
EEERK!
ARGH! IT'S GOING TO BE A REAL SLAUGHTER!
COME AND FIGHT, PUNK!
READY TO ARM WRESTLE, LOSER?
NNNNNNG...
YEAH! YOU'RE GOING TO CRY FOR YOUR MOTHER!
WHAT A ROTTEN FIGHT!
WHATEVER!
PLUMERI & BLOZ - GUEST STAR IDÉE R.ALLAIN

SALTASAURUS

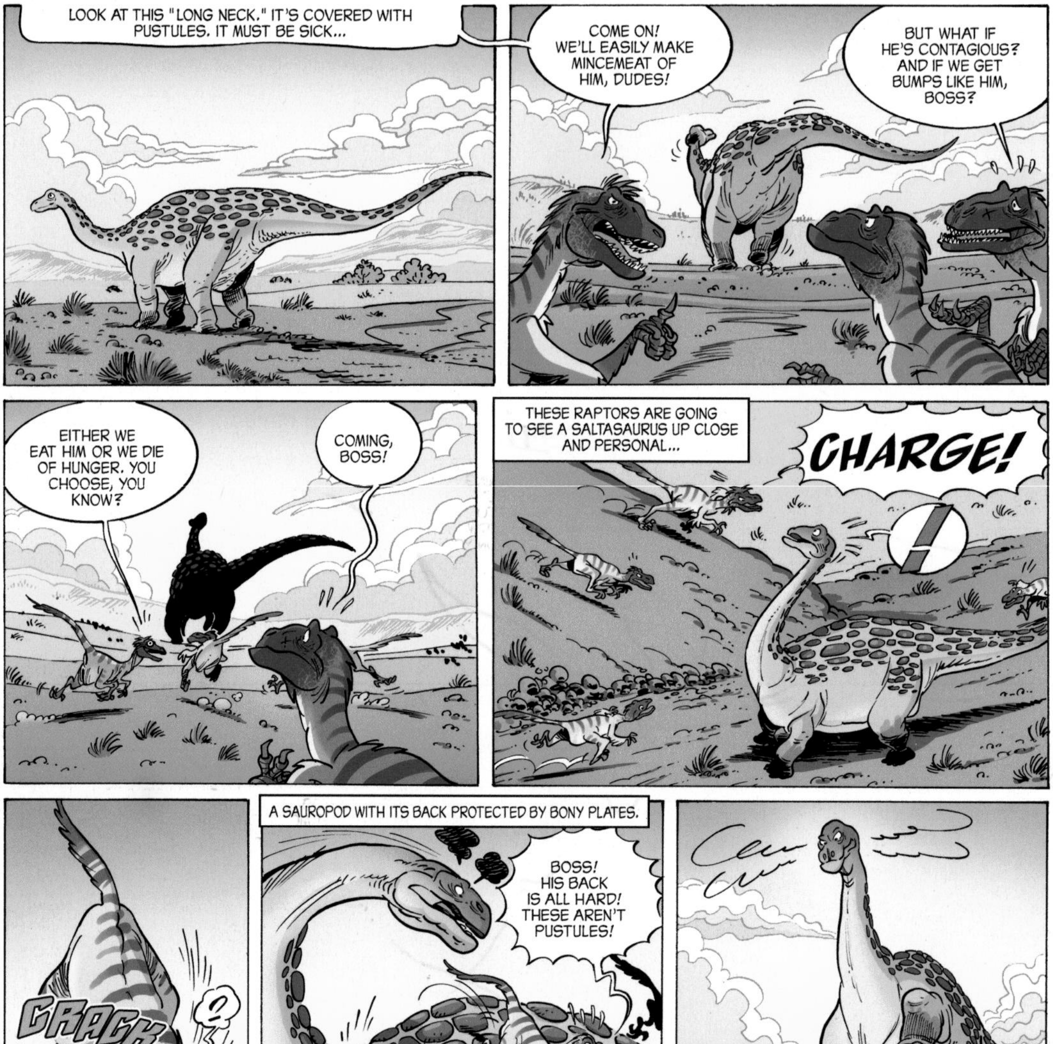
LOOK AT THIS "LONG NECK." IT'S COVERED WITH PUSTULES. IT MUST BE SICK...
COME ON! WE'LL EASILY MAKE MINCEMEAT OF HIM, DUDES!
BUT WHAT IF HE'S CONTAGIOUS? AND IF WE GET BUMPS LIKE HIM, BOSS?
EITHER WE EAT HIM OR WE DIE OF HUNGER. YOU CHOOSE, YOU KNOW?
COMING, BOSS!
THESE RAPTORS ARE GOING TO SEE A SALTASAURUS UP CLOSE AND PERSONAL...
CHARGE!
CRACK
A SAUROPOD WITH ITS BACK PROTECTED BY BONY PLATES.
BOSS! HIS BACK IS ALL HARD! THESE AREN'T PUSTULES!

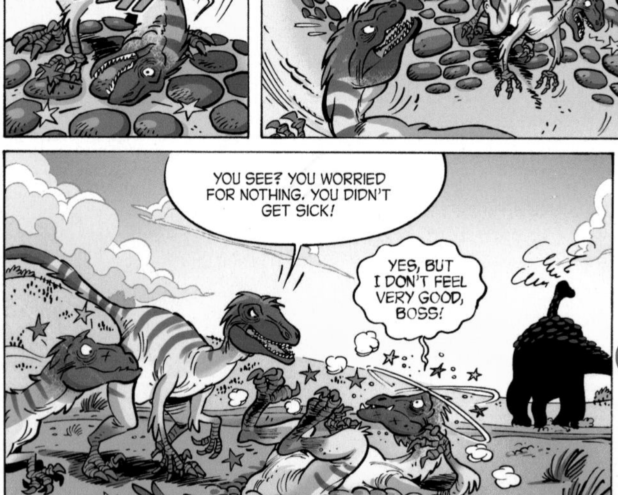
YOU SEE? YOU WORRIED FOR NOTHING. YOU DIDN'T GET SICK!
YES, BUT I DON'T FEEL VERY GOOD, BOSS!

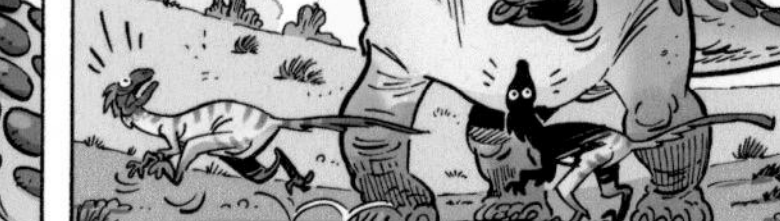

SALTASAURUS

MEANING: LIZARD FROM THE PROVINCE OF SALTA
PERIOD: LATE CRETACEOUS (73-67 MILLION YEARS AGO)
ORDER/ FAMILY: SAURISCHIA/ TITANOSAURIDAE
SIZE: 40 FEET LONG
WEIGHT: 15,000 LBS.
DIET: HERBIVORE
FOUND: ARGENTINA

PLUMERI & BLOZ

COLD-BLOODED OR WARM-BLOODED?

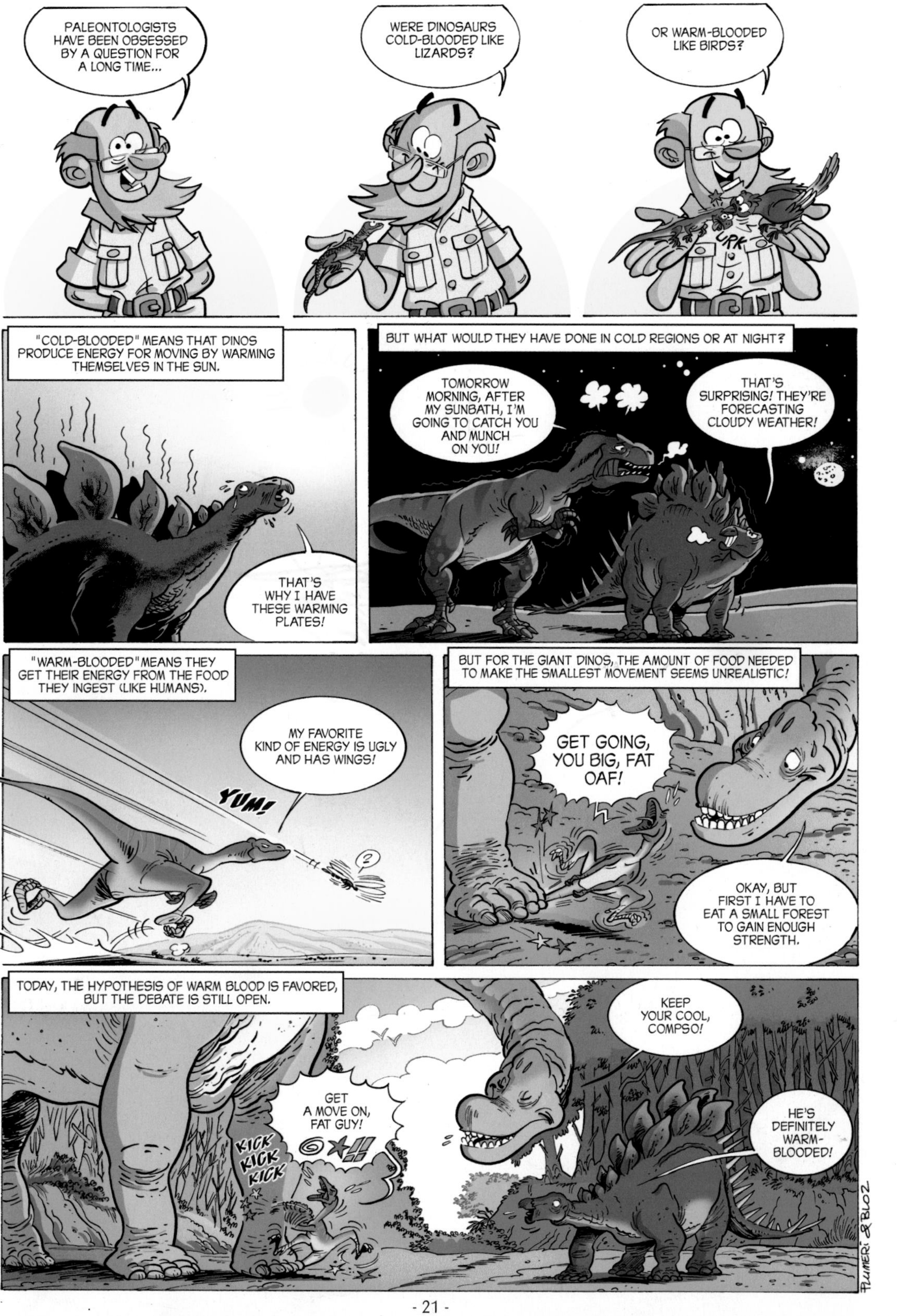

PALEONTOLOGISTS HAVE BEEN OBSESSED BY A QUESTION FOR A LONG TIME...
WERE DINOSAURS COLD-BLOODED LIKE LIZARDS?
OR WARM-BLOODED LIKE BIRDS?
URK
"COLD-BLOODED" MEANS THAT DINOS PRODUCE ENERGY FOR MOVING BY WARMING THEMSELVES IN THE SUN.
THAT'S WHY I HAVE THESE WARMING PLATES!
BUT WHAT WOULD THEY HAVE DONE IN COLD REGIONS OR AT NIGHT?
TOMORROW MORNING, AFTER MY SUNBATH, I'M GOING TO CATCH YOU AND MUNCH ON YOU!
THAT'S SURPRISING! THEY'RE FORECASTING CLOUDY WEATHER!
"WARM-BLOODED" MEANS THEY GET THEIR ENERGY FROM THE FOOD THEY INGEST (LIKE HUMANS).
MY FAVORITE KIND OF ENERGY IS UGLY AND HAS WINGS!
YUM!
?
BUT FOR THE GIANT DINOS, THE AMOUNT OF FOOD NEEDED TO MAKE THE SMALLEST MOVEMENT SEEMS UNREALISTIC!
GET GOING, YOU BIG, FAT OAF!
OKAY, BUT FIRST I HAVE TO EAT A SMALL FOREST TO GAIN ENOUGH STRENGTH.
TODAY, THE HYPOTHESIS OF WARM BLOOD IS FAVORED, BUT THE DEBATE IS STILL OPEN.
KEEP YOUR COOL, COMPSO!
GET A MOVE ON, FAT GUY!
KICK KICK KICK
HE'S DEFINITELY WARM-BLOODED!
PLUMERI & BLOZ

TRIP TO INDIA

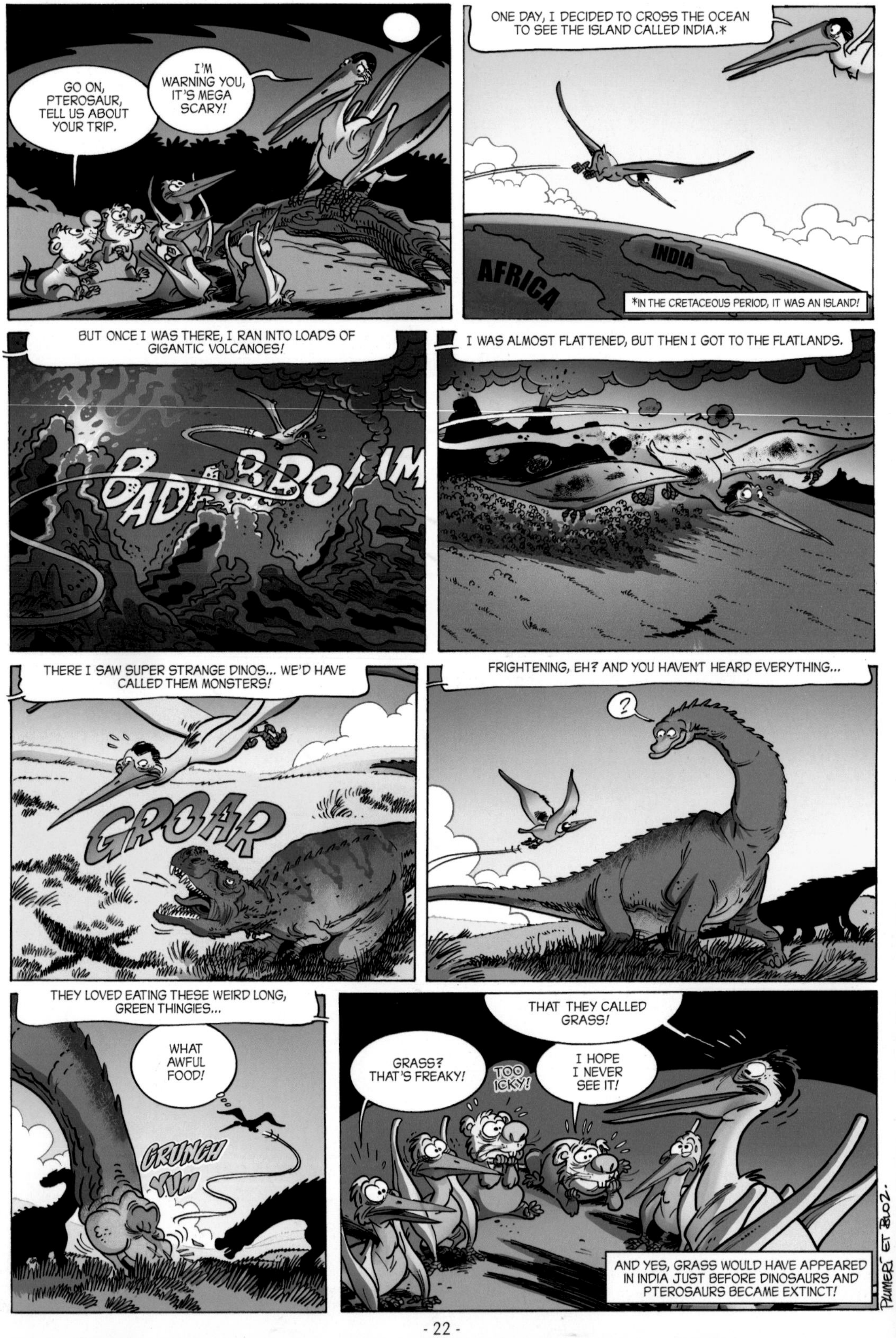
GO ON, PTEROSAUR, TELL US ABOUT YOUR TRIP.
I'M WARNING YOU, IT'S MEGA SCARY!
ONE DAY, I DECIDED TO CROSS THE OCEAN TO SEE THE ISLAND CALLED INDIA.*
INDIA
AFRICA
*IN THE CRETACEOUS PERIOD, IT WAS AN ISLAND!
BUT ONCE I WAS THERE, I RAN INTO LOADS OF GIGANTIC VOLCANOES!
I WAS ALMOST FLATTENED, BUT THEN I GOT TO THE FLATLANDS.
THERE I SAW SUPER STRANGE DINOS... WE'D HAVE CALLED THEM MONSTERS!
GROAR
FRIGHTENING, EH? AND YOU HAVENT HEARD EVERYTHING...
?
THEY LOVED EATING THESE WEIRD LONG, GREEN THINGIES...
WHAT AWFUL FOOD!
CRUNCH
YUM
THAT THEY CALLED GRASS!
GRASS? THAT'S FREAKY!
TOO ICKY!
I HOPE I NEVER SEE IT!
AND YES, GRASS WOULD HAVE APPEARED IN INDIA JUST BEFORE DINOSAURS AND PTEROSAURS BECAME EXTINCT!
PLUMERI ET BLOZ.

PSITTACOSAURUS

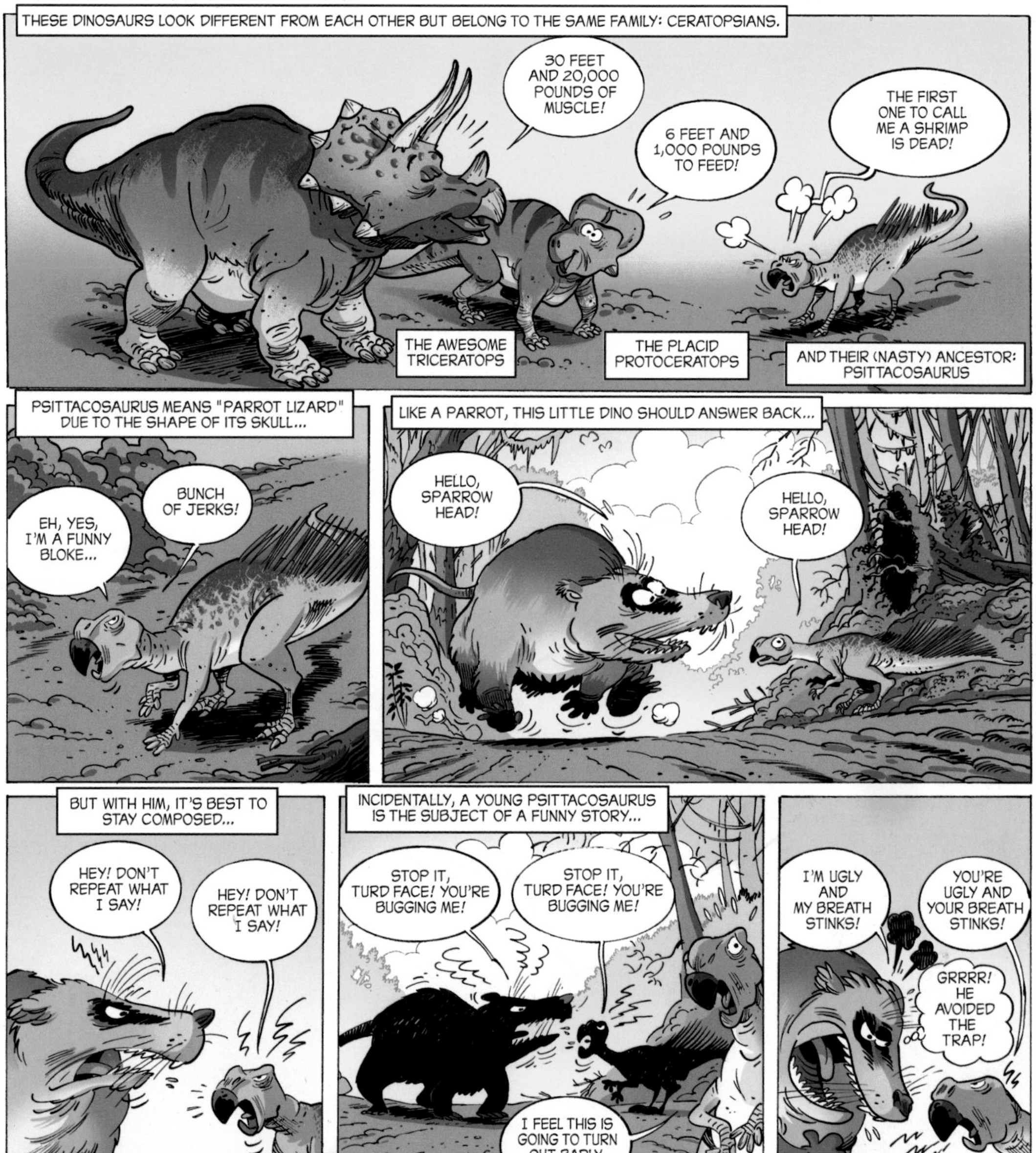

THESE DINOSAURS LOOK DIFFERENT FROM EACH OTHER BUT BELONG TO THE SAME FAMILY: CERATOPSIANS.
30 FEET AND 20,000 POUNDS OF MUSCLE!
6 FEET AND 1,000 POUNDS TO FEED!
THE FIRST ONE TO CALL ME A SHRIMP IS DEAD!
THE AWESOME TRICERATOPS
THE PLACID PROTOCERATOPS
AND THEIR (NASTY) ANCESTOR: PSITTACOSAURUS
PSITTACOSAURUS MEANS "PARROT LIZARD" DUE TO THE SHAPE OF ITS SKULL...
EH, YES, I'M A FUNNY BLOKE...
BUNCH OF JERKS!
LIKE A PARROT, THIS LITTLE DINO SHOULD ANSWER BACK...
HELLO, SPARROW HEAD!
HELLO, SPARROW HEAD!
BUT WITH HIM, IT'S BEST TO STAY COMPOSED...
HEY! DON'T REPEAT WHAT I SAY!
HEY! DON'T REPEAT WHAT I SAY!
INCIDENTALLY, A YOUNG PSITTACOSAURUS IS THE SUBJECT OF A FUNNY STORY...
STOP IT, TURD FACE! YOU'RE BUGGING ME!
STOP IT, TURD FACE! YOU'RE BUGGING ME!
I FEEL THIS IS GOING TO TURN OUT BADLY.
I'M UGLY AND MY BREATH STINKS!
YOU'RE UGLY AND YOUR BREATH STINKS!
GRRRR! HE AVOIDED THE TRAP!

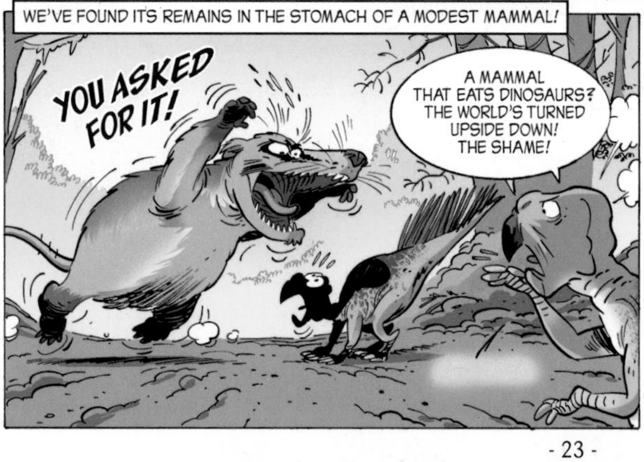

WE'VE FOUND ITS REMAINS IN THE STOMACH OF A MODEST MAMMAL!
YOU ASKED FOR IT!
A MAMMAL THAT EATS DINOSAURS? THE WORLD'S TURNED UPSIDE DOWN! THE SHAME!

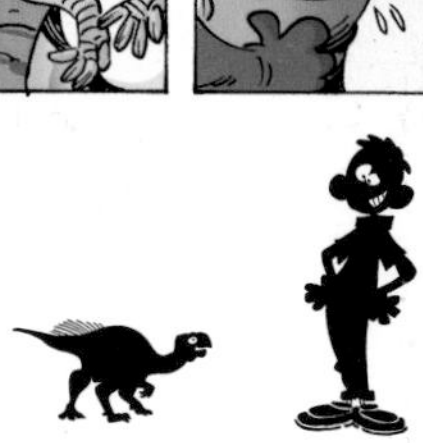

PSITTACOSAURUS

MEANING: PARROT LIZARD
PERIOD: EARLY CRETACEOUS (130-100 MILLION YEARS AGO)
ORDER/ FAMILY: ORNITHISCHIA/ PSITTACOSAURIDAE
SIZE: 7 FEET LONG
WEIGHT: 44 LBS.
DIET: HERBIVORE
FOUND: CHINA, MONGOLIA, RUSSIA

PLUMERI + BLOZ

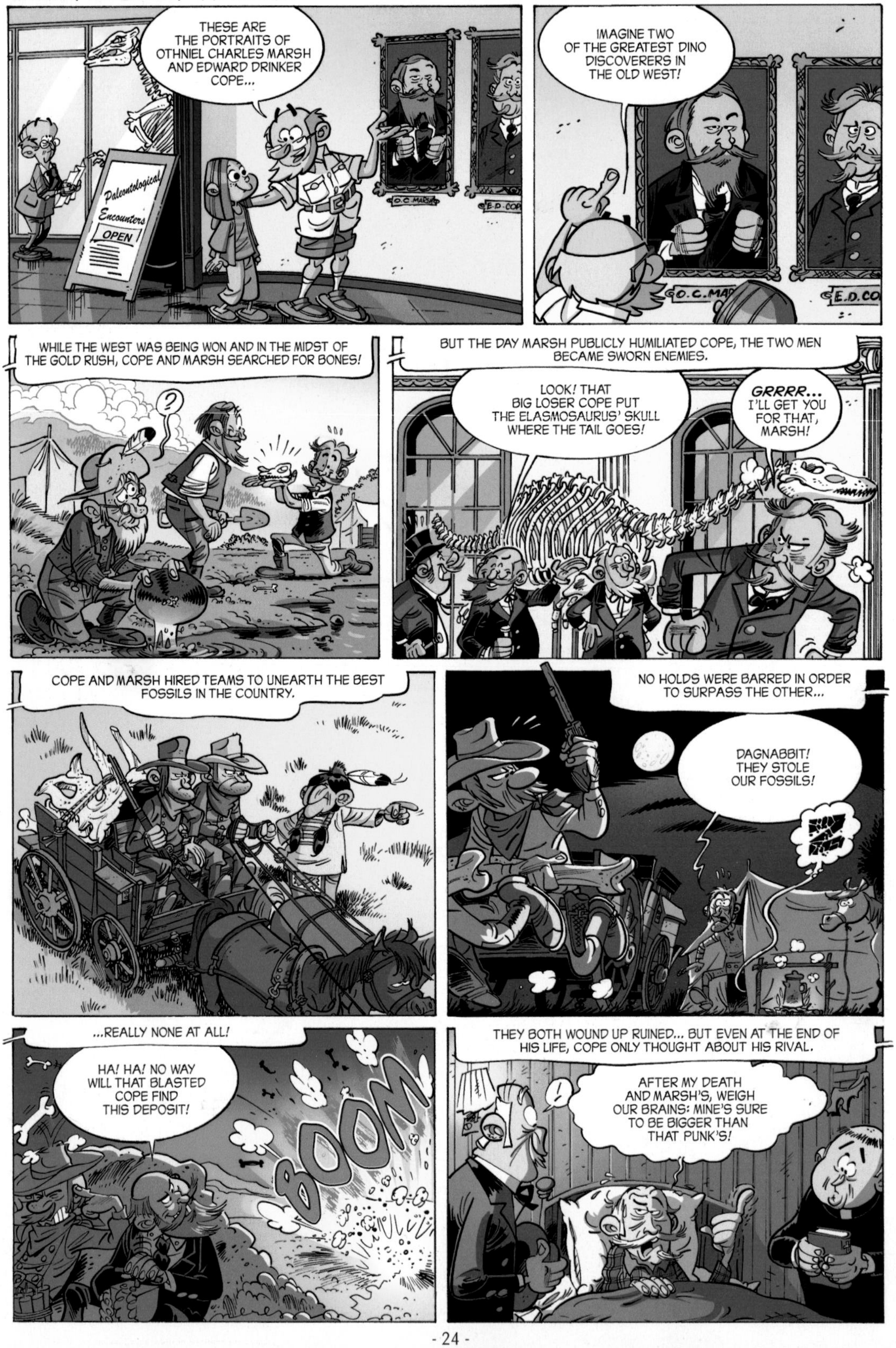
THESE ARE THE PORTRAITS OF OTHNIEL CHARLES MARSH AND EDWARD DRINKER COPE...
Paleontological Encounters
OPEN
O.C.MARSH
E.D.COPE
IMAGINE TWO OF THE GREATEST DINO DISCOVERERS IN THE OLD WEST!
O.C.MAR
E.D.CO
WHILE THE WEST WAS BEING WON AND IN THE MIDST OF THE GOLD RUSH, COPE AND MARSH SEARCHED FOR BONES!
?
BUT THE DAY MARSH PUBLICLY HUMILIATED COPE, THE TWO MEN BECAME SWORN ENEMIES.
LOOK! THAT BIG LOSER COPE PUT THE ELASMOSAURUS' SKULL WHERE THE TAIL GOES!
GRRRR... I'LL GET YOU FOR THAT, MARSH!
COPE AND MARSH HIRED TEAMS TO UNEARTH THE BEST FOSSILS IN THE COUNTRY.
NO HOLDS WERE BARRED IN ORDER TO SURPASS THE OTHER...
DAGNABBIT! THEY STOLE OUR FOSSILS!
...REALLY NONE AT ALL!
HA! HA! NO WAY WILL THAT BLASTED COPE FIND THIS DEPOSIT!
BOOM
THEY BOTH WOUND UP RUINED... BUT EVEN AT THE END OF HIS LIFE, COPE ONLY THOUGHT ABOUT HIS RIVAL.
!
AFTER MY DEATH AND MARSH'S, WEIGH OUR BRAINS: MINE'S SURE TO BE BIGGER THAN THAT PUNK'S!

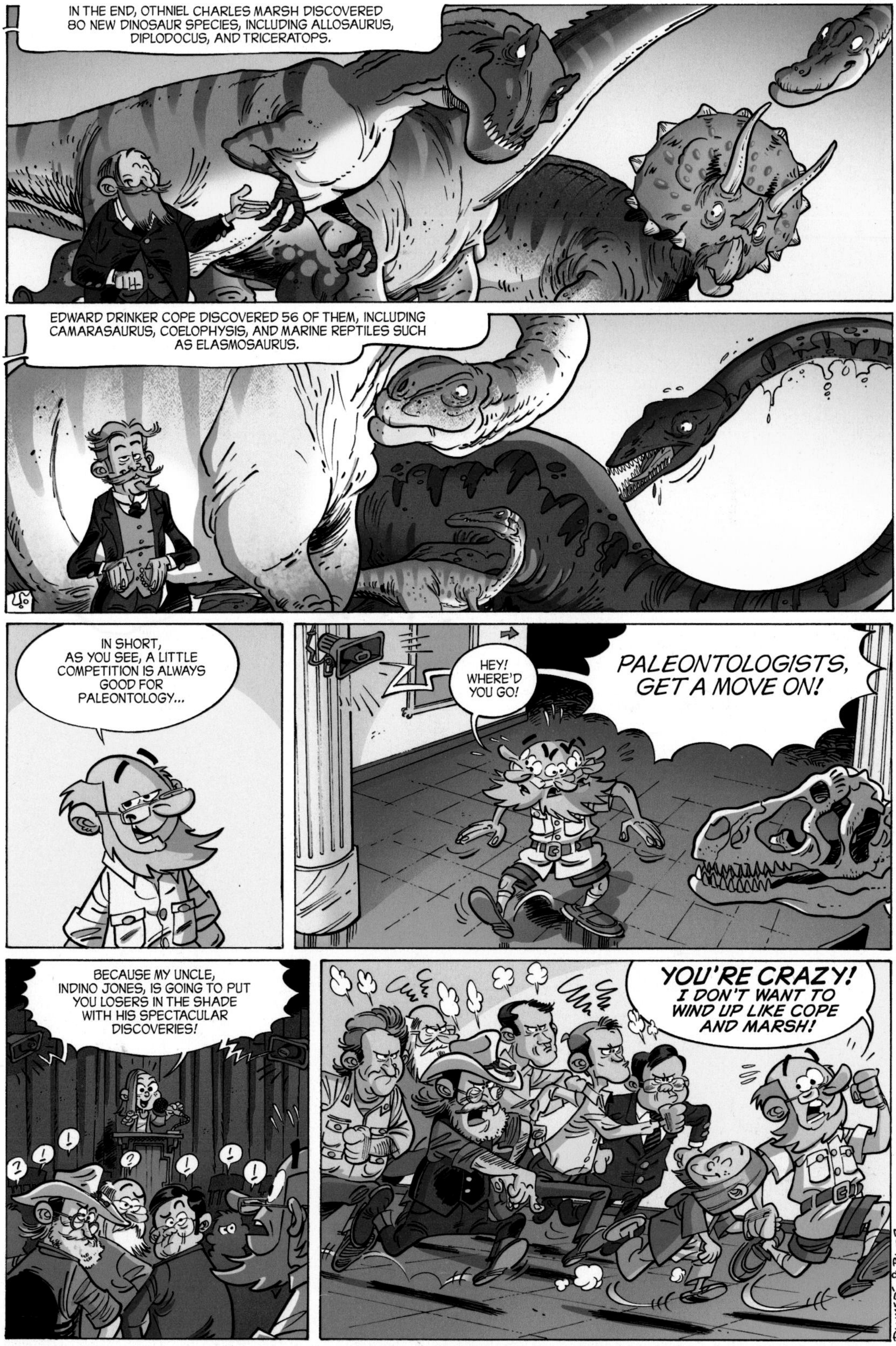

IN THE END, OTHNIEL CHARLES MARSH DISCOVERED 80 NEW DINOSAUR SPECIES, INCLUDING ALLOSAURUS, DIPLODOCUS, AND TRICERATOPS.
EDWARD DRINKER COPE DISCOVERED 56 OF THEM, INCLUDING CAMARASAURUS, COELOPHYSIS, AND MARINE REPTILES SUCH AS ELASMOSAURUS.
IN SHORT, AS YOU SEE, A LITTLE COMPETITION IS ALWAYS GOOD FOR PALEONTOLOGY...
HEY! WHERE'D YOU GO!
PALEONTOLOGISTS, GET A MOVE ON!
BECAUSE MY UNCLE, INDINO JONES, IS GOING TO PUT YOU LOSERS IN THE SHADE WITH HIS SPECTACULAR DISCOVERIES!
YOU'RE CRAZY! I DON'T WANT TO WIND UP LIKE COPE AND MARSH!
PLUMERI & BLOZ

THERIZINOSAURUS'S CLAWS

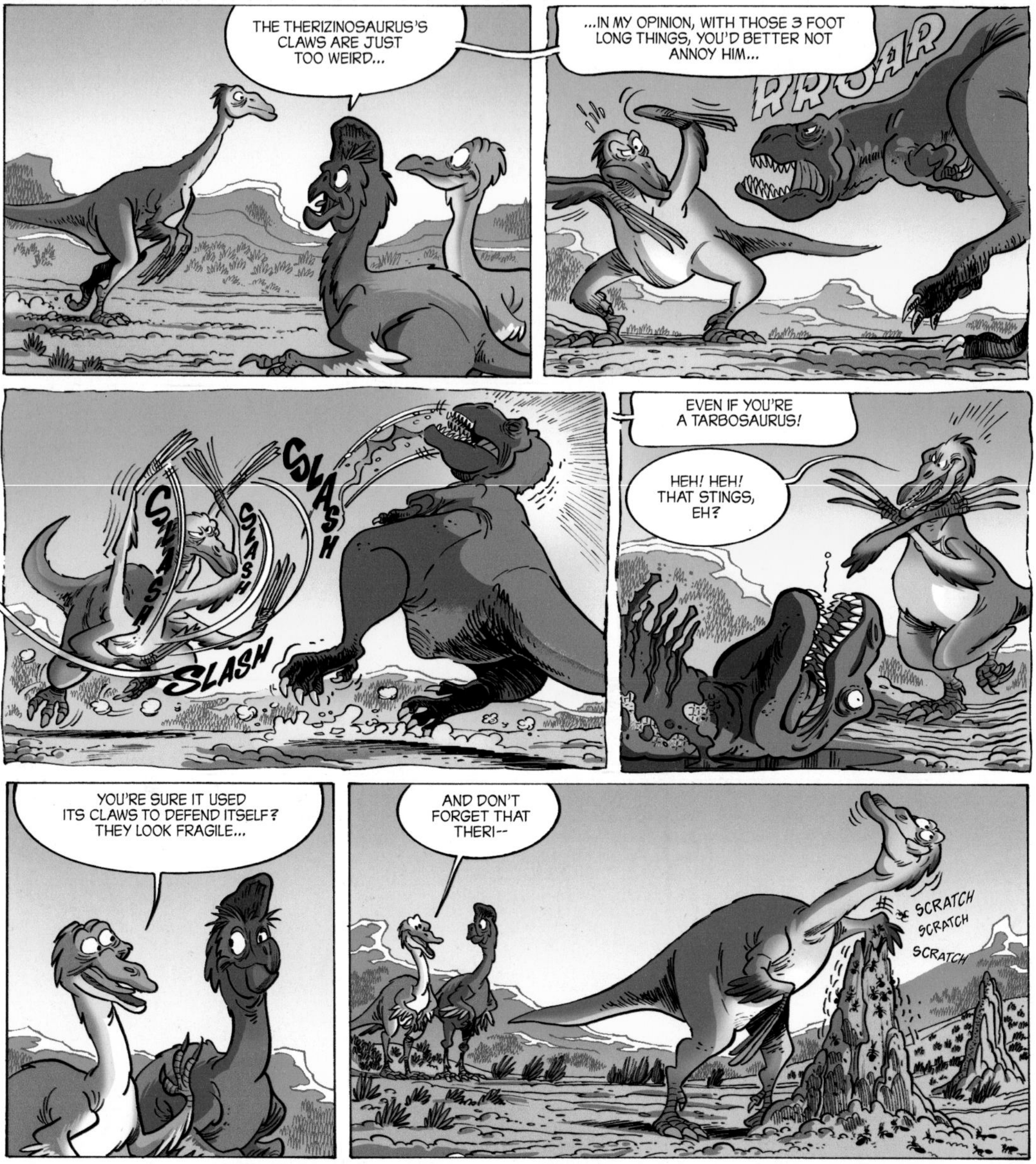

THE THERIZINOSAURUS'S CLAWS ARE JUST TOO WEIRD...
...IN MY OPINION, WITH THOSE 3 FOOT LONG THINGS, YOU'D BETTER NOT ANNOY HIM...
RRROAR
SLASH
SLASH
SLASH
SLASH
SLASH
EVEN IF YOU'RE A TARBOSAURUS!
HEH! HEH! THAT STINGS, EH?
YOU'RE SURE IT USED ITS CLAWS TO DEFEND ITSELF? THEY LOOK FRAGILE...
AND DON'T FORGET THAT THERI--
SCRATCH
SCRATCH
SCRATCH
--IS, FIRST AND FOREMOST, A BIG BELLY ON LEGS!
HEY, GUYS! WHICH DO YOU LIKE BETTER? ANTS OR SURPRISE KEBABS?

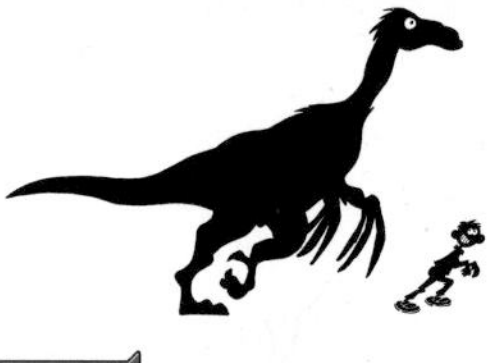

THERIZINOSAURUS

MEANING: SCYTHE LIZARD
PERIOD: LATE CRETACEOUS (70-65 MILLION YEARS AGO)
ORDER/ FAMILY: SAURISCHIA/ THERIZINOSAURIDAE
SIZE: 30 FEET LONG
WEIGHT: 13,000 LBS.
DIET: HERBIVORE
FOUND: CHINA, MONGOLIA

PLUMERI & BLOZ

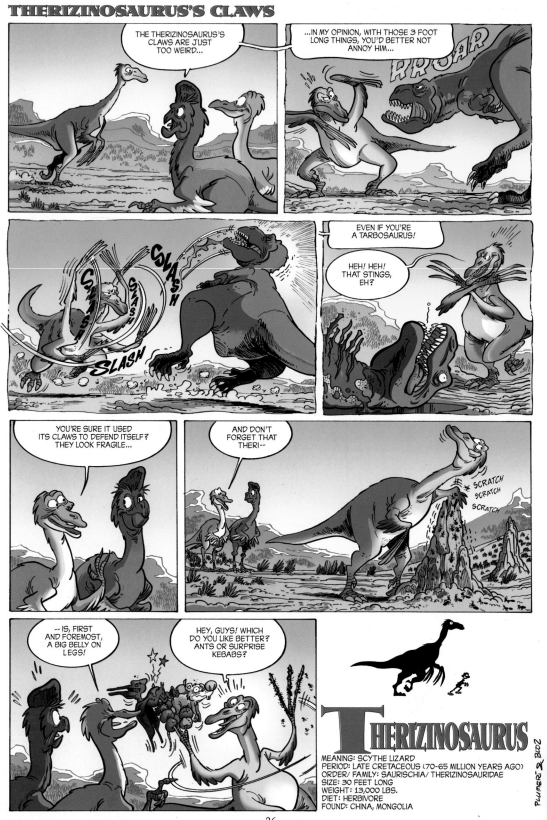

DUCK-BILLED DINOSAURS

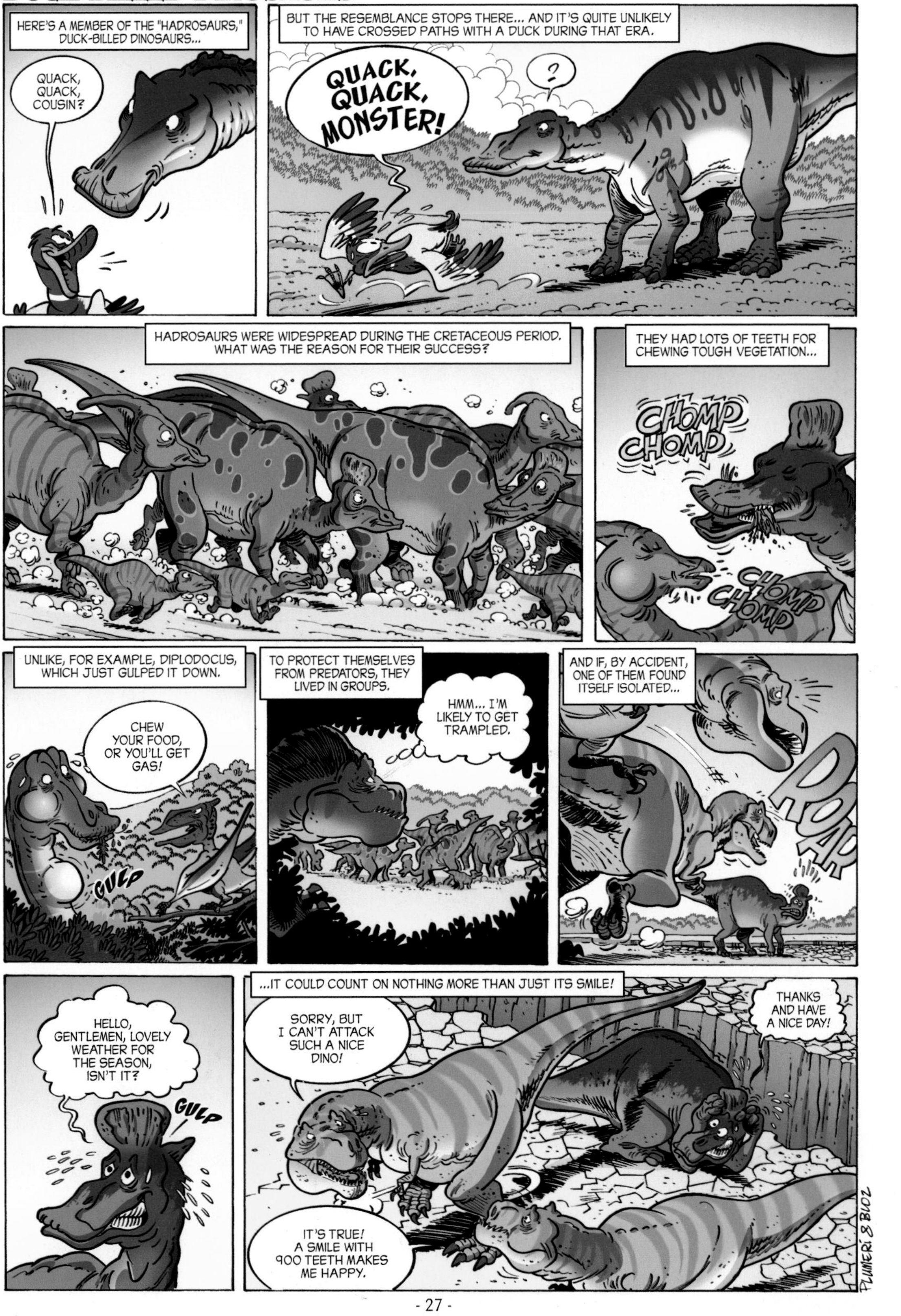
HERE'S A MEMBER OF THE "HADROSAURS," DUCK-BILLED DINOSAURS...
QUACK, QUACK, COUSIN?
BUT THE RESEMBLANCE STOPS THERE... AND IT'S QUITE UNLIKELY TO HAVE CROSSED PATHS WITH A DUCK DURING THAT ERA.
QUACK, QUACK, MONSTER!
?
HADROSAURS WERE WIDESPREAD DURING THE CRETACEOUS PERIOD. WHAT WAS THE REASON FOR THEIR SUCCESS?
THEY HAD LOTS OF TEETH FOR CHEWING TOUGH VEGETATION...
CHOMP CHOMP
CHOMP CHOMP
UNLIKE, FOR EXAMPLE, DIPLODOCUS, WHICH JUST GULPED IT DOWN.
CHEW YOUR FOOD, OR YOU'LL GET GAS!
GULP
TO PROTECT THEMSELVES FROM PREDATORS, THEY LIVED IN GROUPS.
HMM... I'M LIKELY TO GET TRAMPLED.
AND IF, BY ACCIDENT, ONE OF THEM FOUND ITSELF ISOLATED...
ROAR
HELLO, GENTLEMEN, LOVELY WEATHER FOR THE SEASON, ISN'T IT?
GULP
...IT COULD COUNT ON NOTHING MORE THAN JUST ITS SMILE!
SORRY, BUT I CAN'T ATTACK SUCH A NICE DINO!
THANKS AND HAVE A NICE DAY!
IT'S TRUE! A SMILE WITH 900 TEETH MAKES ME HAPPY.
PLUMERI & BLOZ

COMPSOGNATHUS HUNTERS (1)

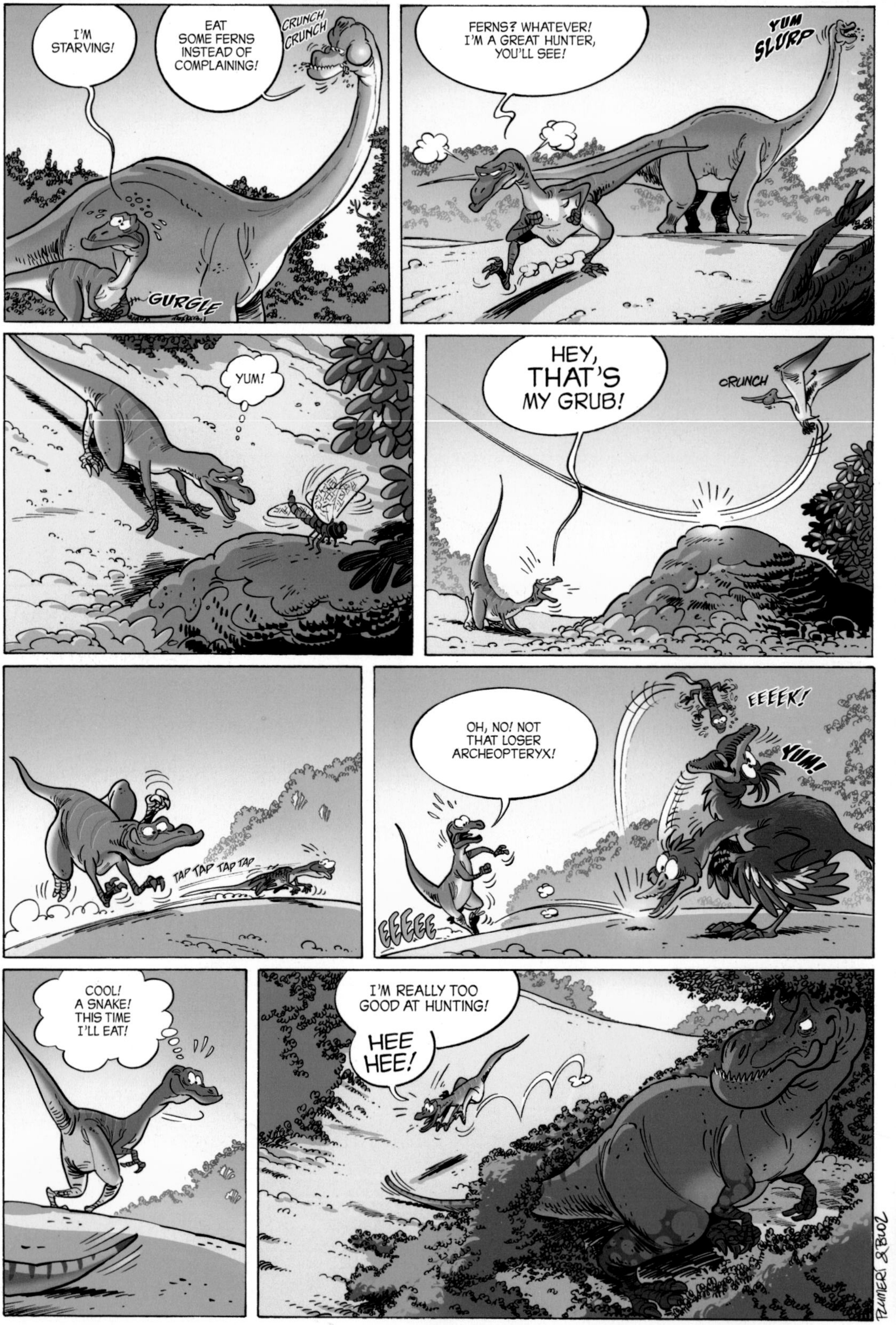
I'M STARVING!
EAT SOME FERNS INSTEAD OF COMPLAINING!
CRUNCH CRUNCH
GURGLE
FERNS? WHATEVER! I'M A GREAT HUNTER, YOU'LL SEE!
YUM SLURP
YUM!
HEY, THAT'S MY GRUB!
CRUNCH
TAP TAP TAP TAP
OH, NO! NOT THAT LOSER ARCHEOPTERYX!
EEEEK!
YUM!
EEEEE
COOL! A SNAKE! THIS TIME I'LL EAT!
I'M REALLY TOO GOOD AT HUNTING!
HEE HEE!
PLUMERI &BLOZ

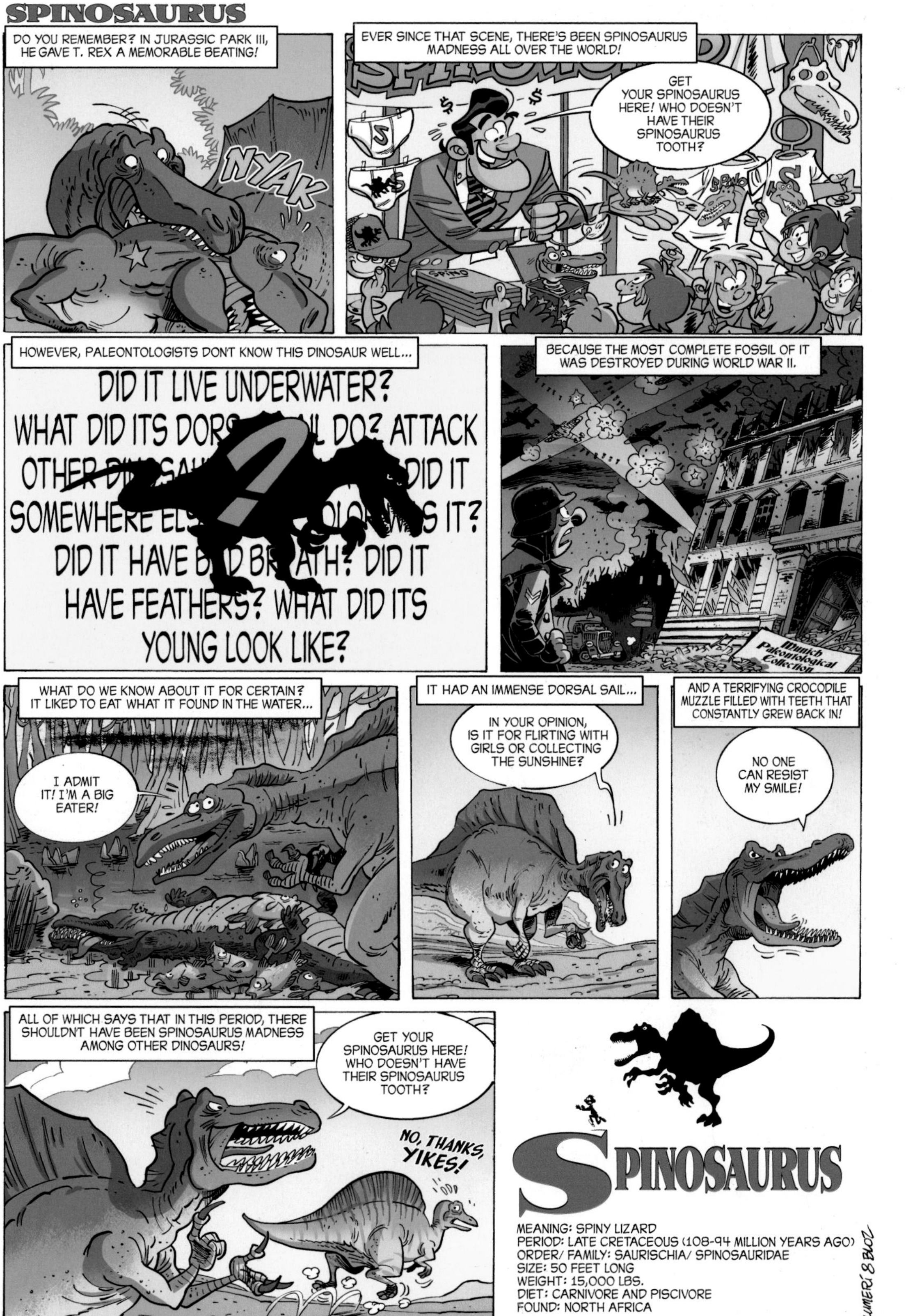
SPINOSAURUS
DO YOU REMEMBER? IN JURASSIC PARK III, HE GAVE T. REX A MEMORABLE BEATING!
NYAK
EVER SINCE THAT SCENE, THERE'S BEEN SPINOSAURUS MADNESS ALL OVER THE WORLD!
GET YOUR SPINOSAURUS HERE! WHO DOESN'T HAVE THEIR SPINOSAURUS TOOTH?
SPINO
HOWEVER, PALEONTOLOGISTS DON'T KNOW THIS DINOSAUR WELL...
DID IT LIVE UNDERWATER?
WHAT DID ITS DORS IL DO? ATTACK
OTHER DID IT
SOMEWHERE ELS COLOR S IT?
DID IT HAVE B D BR ATH? DID IT
HAVE FEATHERS? WHAT DID ITS
YOUNG LOOK LIKE?
BECAUSE THE MOST COMPLETE FOSSIL OF IT WAS DESTROYED DURING WORLD WAR II.
Munich Paleontological Collection
WHAT DO WE KNOW ABOUT IT FOR CERTAIN? IT LIKED TO EAT WHAT IT FOUND IN THE WATER...
I ADMIT IT! I'M A BIG EATER!
IT HAD AN IMMENSE DORSAL SAIL...
IN YOUR OPINION, IS IT FOR FLIRTING WITH GIRLS OR COLLECTING THE SUNSHINE?
AND A TERRIFYING CROCODILE MUZZLE FILLED WITH TEETH THAT CONSTANTLY GREW BACK IN!
NO ONE CAN RESIST MY SMILE!
ALL OF WHICH SAYS THAT IN THIS PERIOD, THERE SHOULDN'T HAVE BEEN SPINOSAURUS MADNESS AMONG OTHER DINOSAURS!
GET YOUR SPINOSAURUS HERE! WHO DOESN'T HAVE THEIR SPINOSAURUS TOOTH?
NO, THANKS, YIKES!
SPINOSAURUS
MEANING: SPINY LIZARD
PERIOD: LATE CRETACEOUS (108-94 MILLION YEARS AGO)
ORDER/ FAMILY: SAURISCHIA/ SPINOSAURIDAE
SIZE: 50 FEET LONG
WEIGHT: 15,000 LBS.
DIET: CARNIVORE AND PISCIVORE
FOUND: NORTH AFRICA
PLUMERI 8 BLOZ

THE RAPTOR AND THE PTEROSAUR

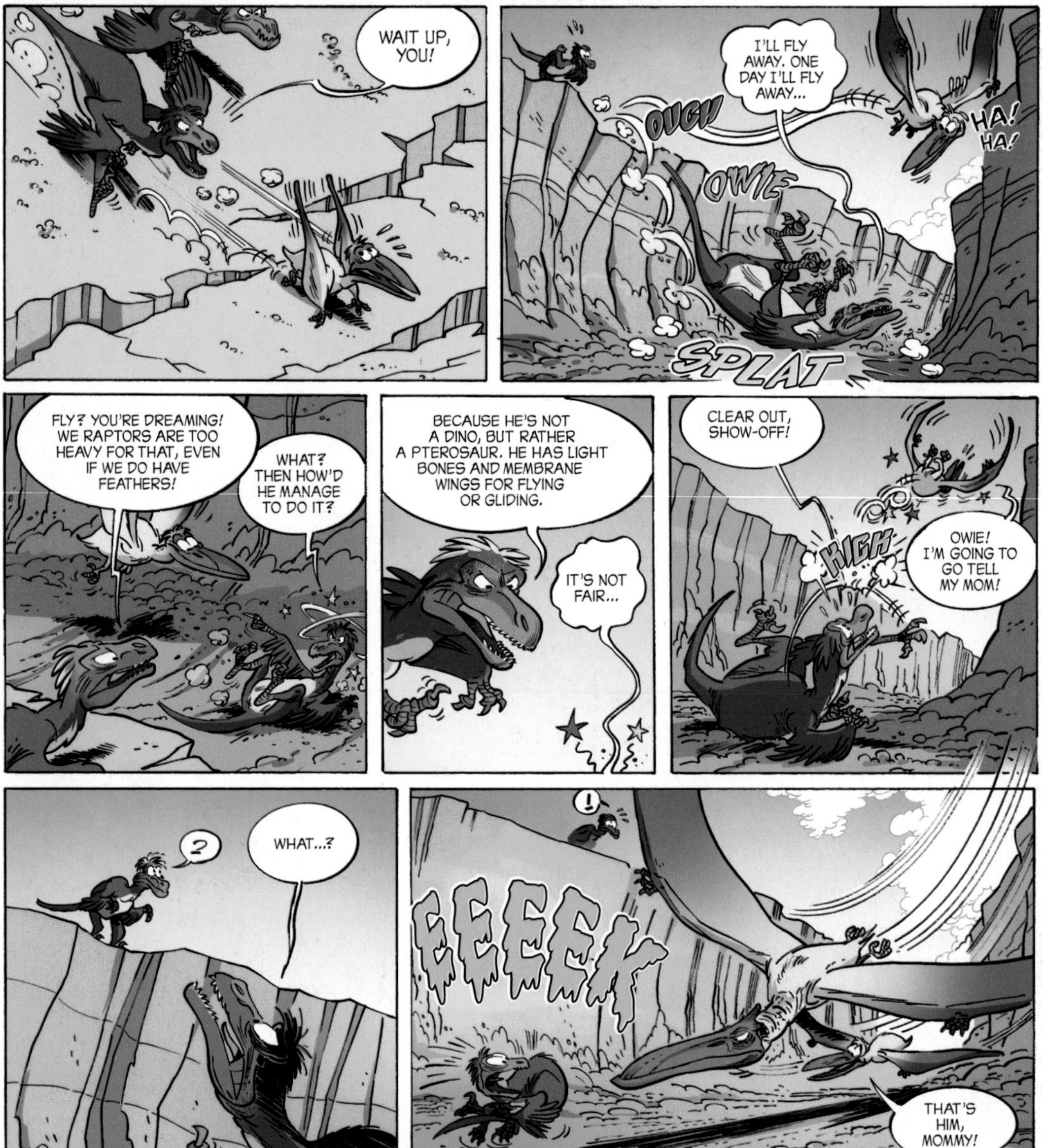
WAIT UP, YOU!
I'LL FLY AWAY. ONE DAY I'LL FLY AWAY...
HA! HA!
OUCH
OWIE
SPLAT
FLY? YOU'RE DREAMING! WE RAPTORS ARE TOO HEAVY FOR THAT, EVEN IF WE DO HAVE FEATHERS!
WHAT? THEN HOW'D HE MANAGE TO DO IT?
BECAUSE HE'S NOT A DINO, BUT RATHER A PTEROSAUR. HE HAS LIGHT BONES AND MEMBRANE WINGS FOR FLYING OR GLIDING.
IT'S NOT FAIR...
CLEAR OUT, SHOW-OFF!
KICK
OWIE! I'M GOING TO GO TELL MY MOM!
?
WHAT...?
!
EEEEK
THAT'S HIM, MOMMY!

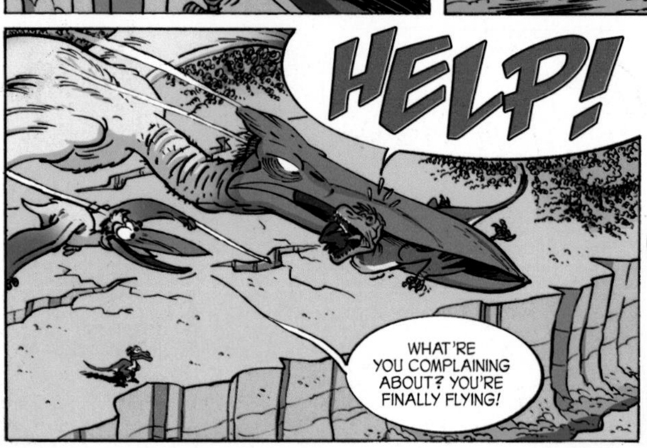
HELP!
WHAT'RE YOU COMPLAINING ABOUT? YOU'RE FINALLY FLYING!

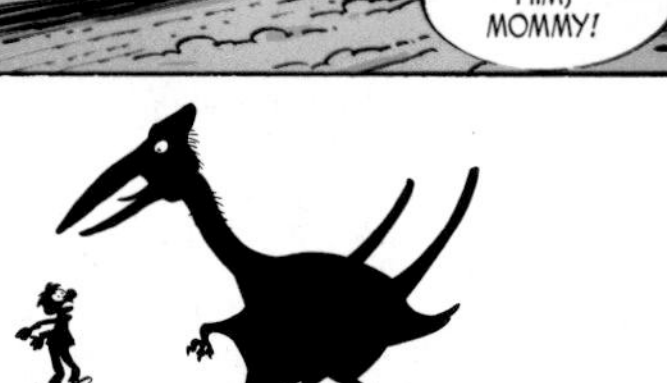

QUETZALCOATLUS

MEANING: NAMED AFTER THE SERPENT GOD, QUETZALCOATL
PERIOD: LATE CRETACEOUS (70-65 MILLION YEARS AGO)
ORDER/ FAMILY: PTEROSAURIA/ AZHDARCHIDAE
SIZE: 33 FOOT WINGSPAN
WEIGHT: 250 LBS.
DIET: PISCIVORE, CARNIVORE?
FOUND: NORTH AMERICA

GIZZARD STONES

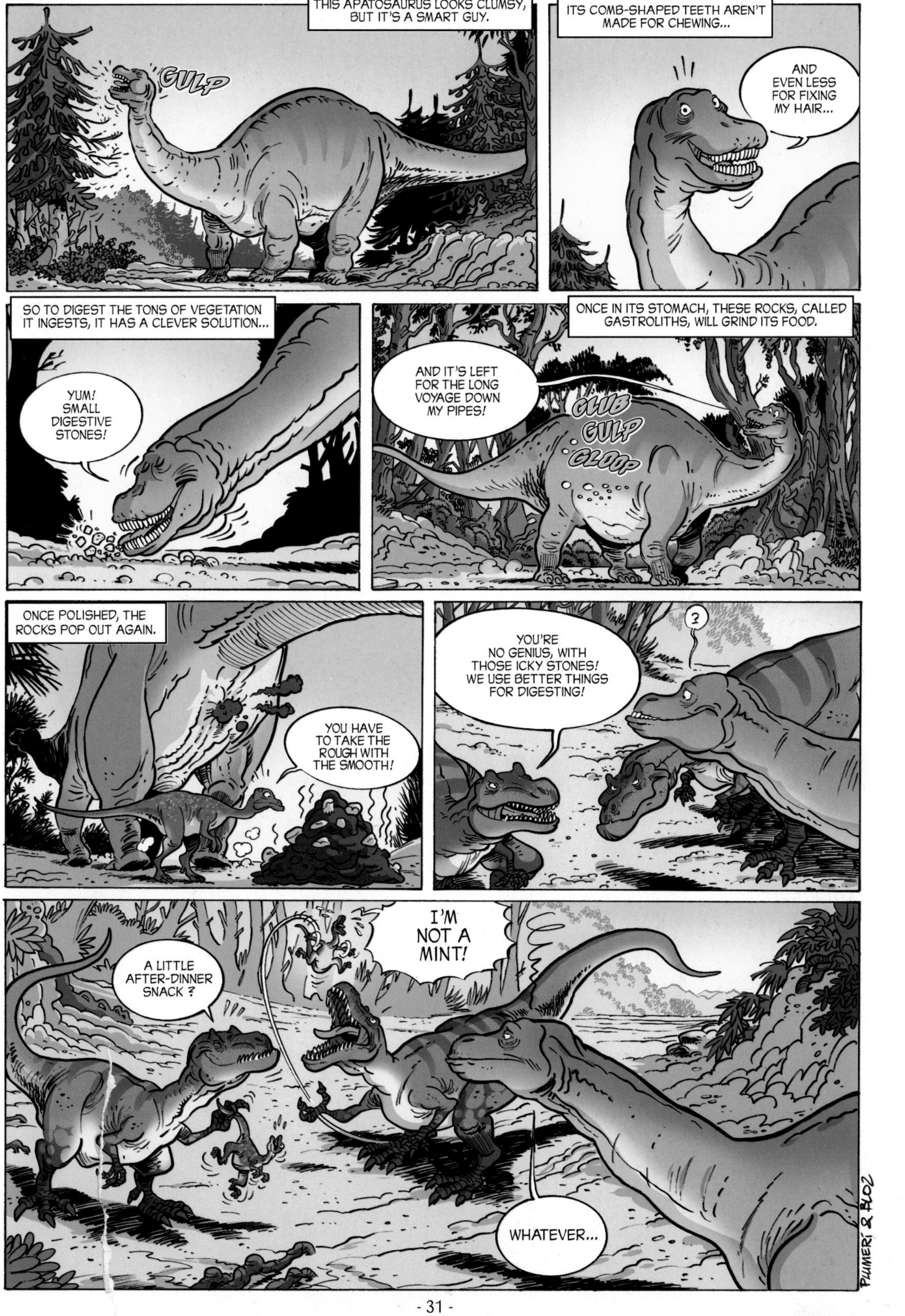

THIS APATOSAURUS LOOKS CLUMSY, BUT IT'S A SMART GUY.
GULP
ITS COMB-SHAPED TEETH AREN'T MADE FOR CHEWING...
AND EVEN LESS FOR FIXING MY HAIR...
SO TO DIGEST THE TONS OF VEGETATION IT INGESTS, IT HAS A CLEVER SOLUTION...
YUM! SMALL DIGESTIVE STONES!
ONCE IN ITS STOMACH, THESE ROCKS, CALLED GASTROLITHS, WILL GRIND ITS FOOD.
AND IT'S LEFT FOR THE LONG VOYAGE DOWN MY PIPES!
GLUB
GULP
GLOOP
ONCE POLISHED, THE ROCKS POP OUT AGAIN.
YOU HAVE TO TAKE THE ROUGH WITH THE SMOOTH!
YOU'RE NO GENIUS, WITH THOSE ICKY STONES! WE USE BETTER THINGS FOR DIGESTING!
?
A LITTLE AFTER-DINNER SNACK ?
I'M NOT A MINT!
WHATEVER...
PLUMERI & BLOZ

HOW LONG DID A DINOSAUR LIVE?

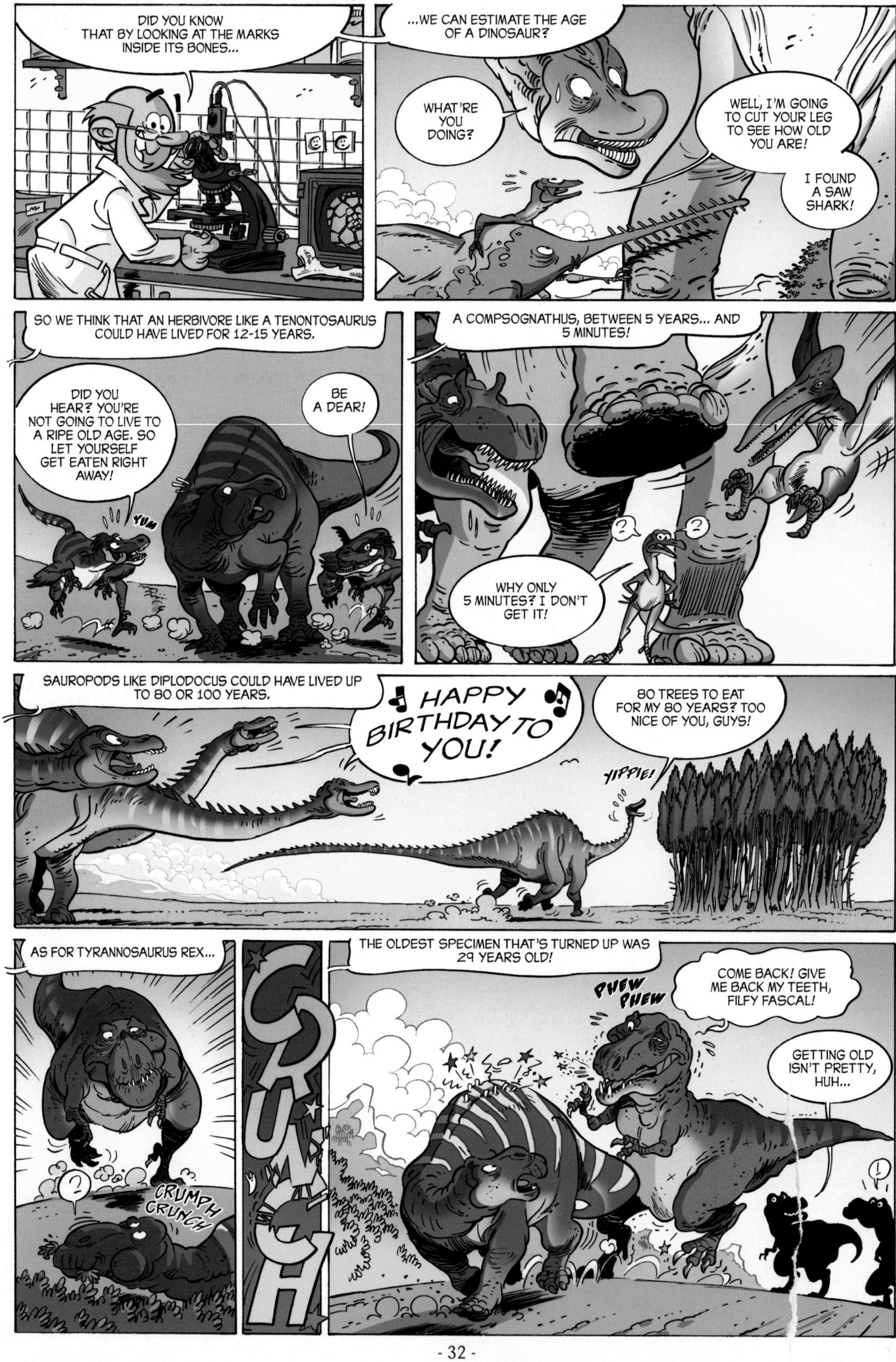
DID YOU KNOW THAT BY LOOKING AT THE MARKS INSIDE ITS BONES...
...WE CAN ESTIMATE THE AGE OF A DINOSAUR?
WHAT'RE YOU DOING?
WELL, I'M GOING TO CUT YOUR LEG TO SEE HOW OLD YOU ARE!
I FOUND A SAW SHARK!
SO WE THINK THAT AN HERBIVORE LIKE A TENONTOSAURUS COULD HAVE LIVED FOR 12-15 YEARS.
DID YOU HEAR? YOU'RE NOT GOING TO LIVE TO A RIPE OLD AGE. SO LET YOURSELF GET EATEN RIGHT AWAY!
BE A DEAR!
YUM
A COMPSOGNATHUS, BETWEEN 5 YEARS... AND 5 MINUTES!
?
?
WHY ONLY 5 MINUTES? I DON'T GET IT!
SAUROPODS LIKE DIPLODOCUS COULD HAVE LIVED UP TO 80 OR 100 YEARS.
HAPPY BIRTHDAY TO YOU!
80 TREES TO EAT FOR MY 80 YEARS? TOO NICE OF YOU, GUYS!
YIPPIE!
AS FOR TYRANNOSAURUS REX...
?
CRUMPH CRUNCH
CRUNCH
THE OLDEST SPECIMEN THAT'S TURNED UP WAS 29 YEARS OLD!
PHEW PHEW
COME BACK! GIVE ME BACK MY TEETH, FILFY FASCAL!
GETTING OLD ISN'T PRETTY, HUH...
!
PLUMERI & BLOZ

T. REX'S PEE

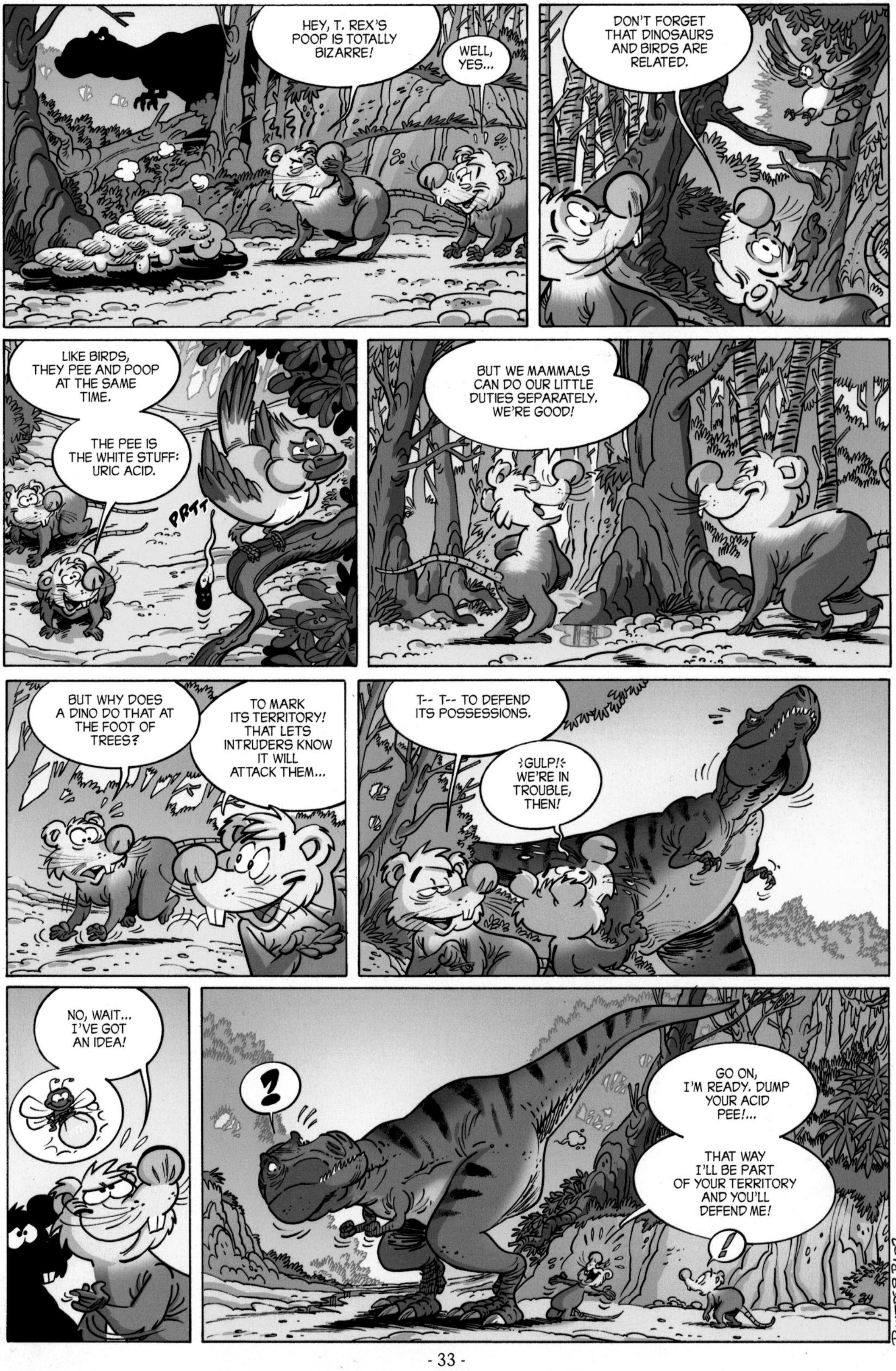

HEY, T. REX'S POOP IS TOTALLY BIZARRE!
WELL, YES...
DON'T FORGET THAT DINOSAURS AND BIRDS ARE RELATED.
LIKE BIRDS, THEY PEE AND POOP AT THE SAME TIME.
THE PEE IS THE WHITE STUFF: URIC ACID.
PRTT
BUT WE MAMMALS CAN DO OUR LITTLE DUTIES SEPARATELY. WE'RE GOOD!
BUT WHY DOES A DINO DO THAT AT THE FOOT OF TREES?
TO MARK ITS TERRITORY! THAT LETS INTRUDERS KNOW IT WILL ATTACK THEM...
T-- T-- TO DEFEND ITS POSSESSIONS.
GULP! WE'RE IN TROUBLE, THEN!
NO, WAIT... I'VE GOT AN IDEA!
?
GO ON, I'M READY. DUMP YOUR ACID PEE!...
THAT WAY I'LL BE PART OF YOUR TERRITORY AND YOU'LL DEFEND ME!
!
PLUMERI & BLOZ

CAMARASAURUS

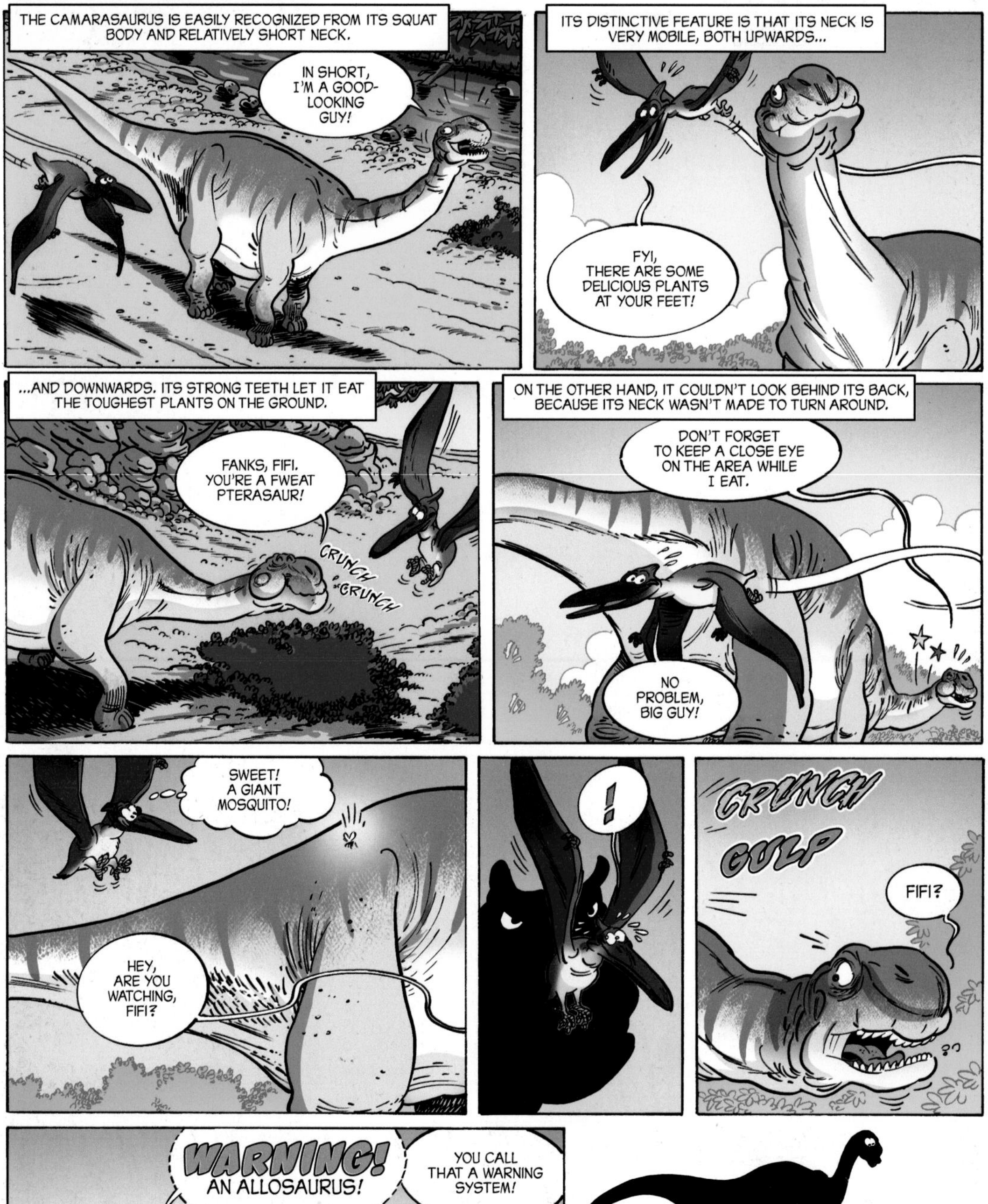
THE CAMARASAURUS IS EASILY RECOGNIZED FROM ITS SQUAT BODY AND RELATIVELY SHORT NECK.
IN SHORT, I'M A GOOD-LOOKING GUY!
ITS DISTINCTIVE FEATURE IS THAT ITS NECK IS VERY MOBILE, BOTH UPWARDS...
FYI, THERE ARE SOME DELICIOUS PLANTS AT YOUR FEET!
...AND DOWNWARDS. ITS STRONG TEETH LET IT EAT THE TOUGHEST PLANTS ON THE GROUND.
FANKS, FIFI. YOU'RE A FWEAT PTERASAUR!
CRUNCH
CRUNCH
ON THE OTHER HAND, IT COULDN'T LOOK BEHIND ITS BACK, BECAUSE ITS NECK WASN'T MADE TO TURN AROUND.
DON'T FORGET TO KEEP A CLOSE EYE ON THE AREA WHILE I EAT.
NO PROBLEM, BIG GUY!
SWEET! A GIANT MOSQUITO!
HEY, ARE YOU WATCHING, FIFI?
!
CRUNCH
GULP
FIFI?

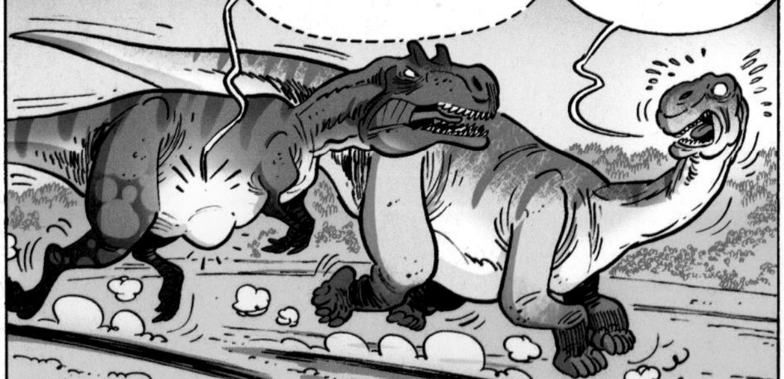
WARNING! AN ALLOSAURUS!
YOU CALL THAT A WARNING SYSTEM!

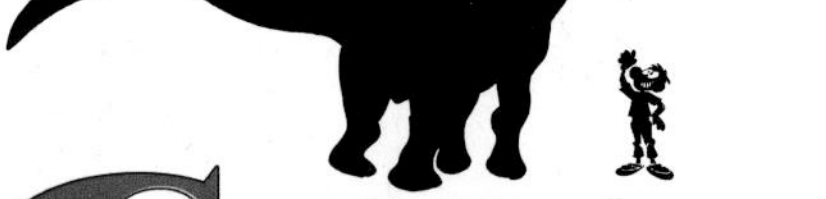

CAMARASAURUS

MEANING: CHAMBERED LIZARD
PERIOD: LATE JURASSIC (155-144 MILLION YEARS AGO)
ORDER/ FAMILY: SAURISCHIA/ CAMARASAURIDAE
SIZE: 75 FEET LONG
WEIGHT: 60,000 LBS.
DIET: HERBIVORE
FOUND: NORTH AMERICA

PLUMERI & BLOZ

WEIRD NAMES

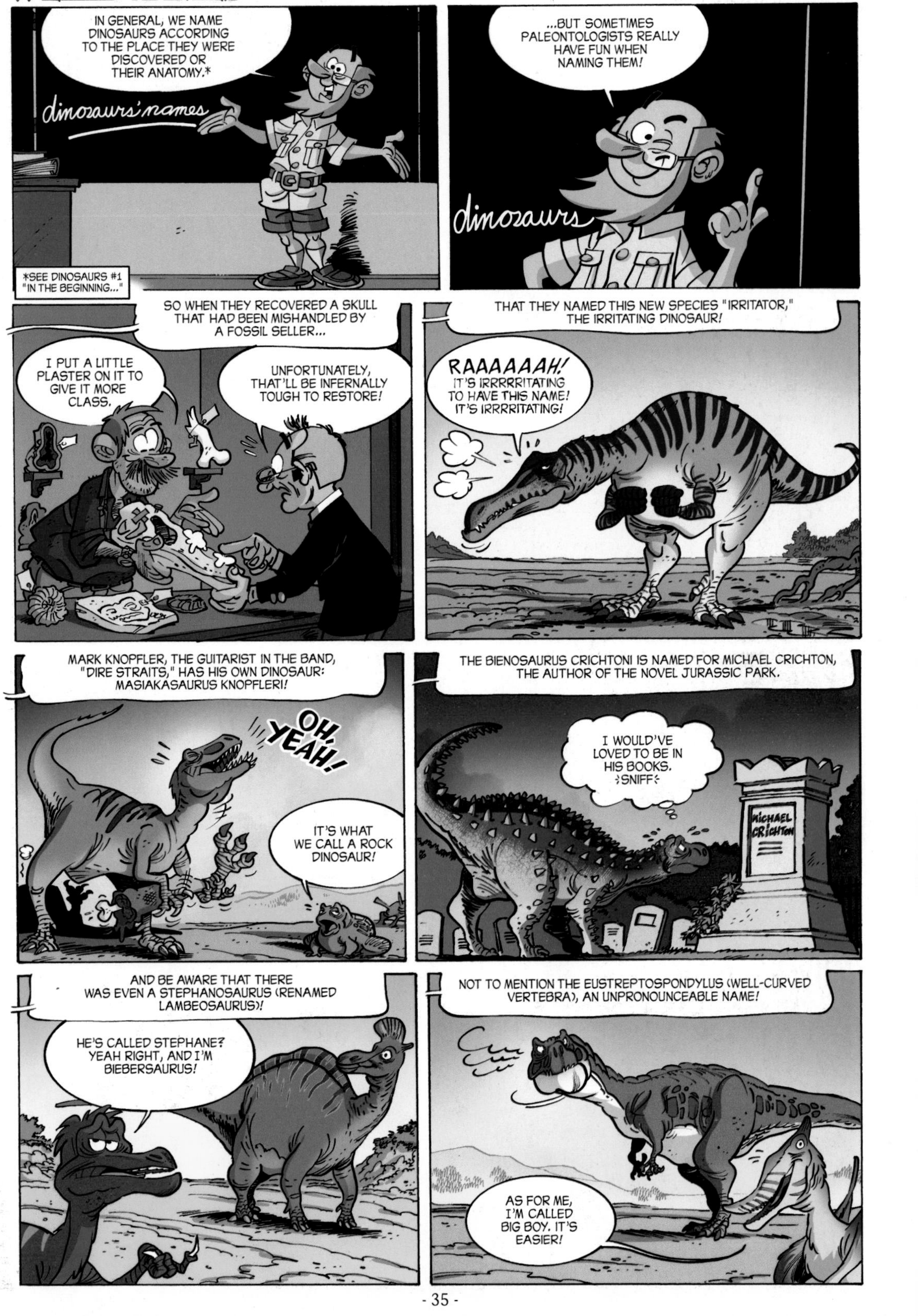

IN GENERAL, WE NAME DINOSAURS ACCORDING TO THE PLACE THEY WERE DISCOVERED OR THEIR ANATOMY.*
dinosaurs' names
*SEE DINOSAURS #1 "IN THE BEGINNING..."
...BUT SOMETIMES PALEONTOLOGISTS REALLY HAVE FUN WHEN NAMING THEM!
dinosaurs
SO WHEN THEY RECOVERED A SKULL THAT HAD BEEN MISHANDLED BY A FOSSIL SELLER...
I PUT A LITTLE PLASTER ON IT TO GIVE IT MORE CLASS.
UNFORTUNATELY, THAT'LL BE INFERNALLY TOUGH TO RESTORE!
THAT THEY NAMED THIS NEW SPECIES "IRRITATOR," THE IRRITATING DINOSAUR!
RAAAAAAH! IT'S IRRRRRITATING TO HAVE THIS NAME! IT'S IRRRRITATING!
MARK KNOPFLER, THE GUITARIST IN THE BAND, "DIRE STRAITS," HAS HIS OWN DINOSAUR: MASIAKASAURUS KNOPFLERI!
OH, YEAH!
IT'S WHAT WE CALL A ROCK DINOSAUR!
THE BIENOSAURUS CRICHTONI IS NAMED FOR MICHAEL CRICHTON, THE AUTHOR OF THE NOVEL JURASSIC PARK.
I WOULD'VE LOVED TO BE IN HIS BOOKS. *SNIFF*
MICHAEL CRICHTON
AND BE AWARE THAT THERE WAS EVEN A STEPHANOSAURUS (RENAMED LAMBEOSAURUS)!
HE'S CALLED STEPHANE? YEAH RIGHT, AND I'M BIEBERSAURUS!
NOT TO MENTION THE EUSTREPTOSPONDYLUS (WELL-CURVED VERTEBRA), AN UNPRONOUNCEABLE NAME!
AS FOR ME, I'M CALLED BIG BOY. IT'S EASIER!

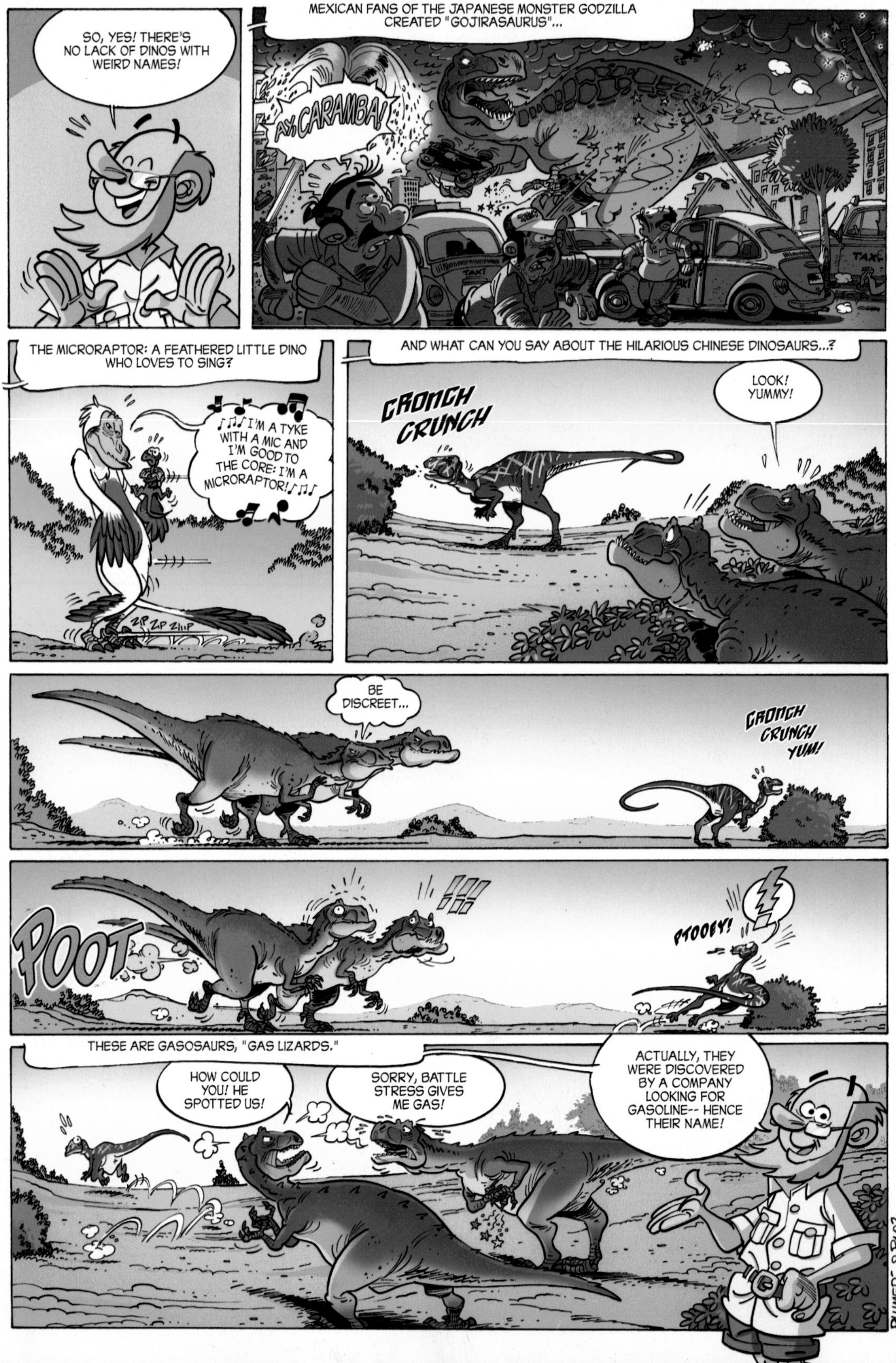
SO, YES! THERE'S NO LACK OF DINOS WITH WEIRD NAMES!
MEXICAN FANS OF THE JAPANESE MONSTER GODZILLA CREATED "GOJIRASAURUS"...
AY, CARAMBA!
TAXI
THE MICRORAPTOR: A FEATHERED LITTLE DINO WHO LOVES TO SING?
I'M A TYKE WITH A MIC AND I'M GOOD TO THE CORE: I'M A MICRORAPTOR!
ZIP ZIP ZIIIP
AND WHAT CAN YOU SAY ABOUT THE HILARIOUS CHINESE DINOSAURS...?
CRONCH CRUNCH
LOOK! YUMMY!
BE DISCREET...
CRONCH CRUNCH YUM!
POOT
PTOOEY!
THESE ARE GASOSAURS, "GAS LIZARDS."
HOW COULD YOU! HE SPOTTED US!
SORRY, BATTLE STRESS GIVES ME GAS!
ACTUALLY, THEY WERE DISCOVERED BY A COMPANY LOOKING FOR GASOLINE-- HENCE THEIR NAME!

CONCAVENATOR

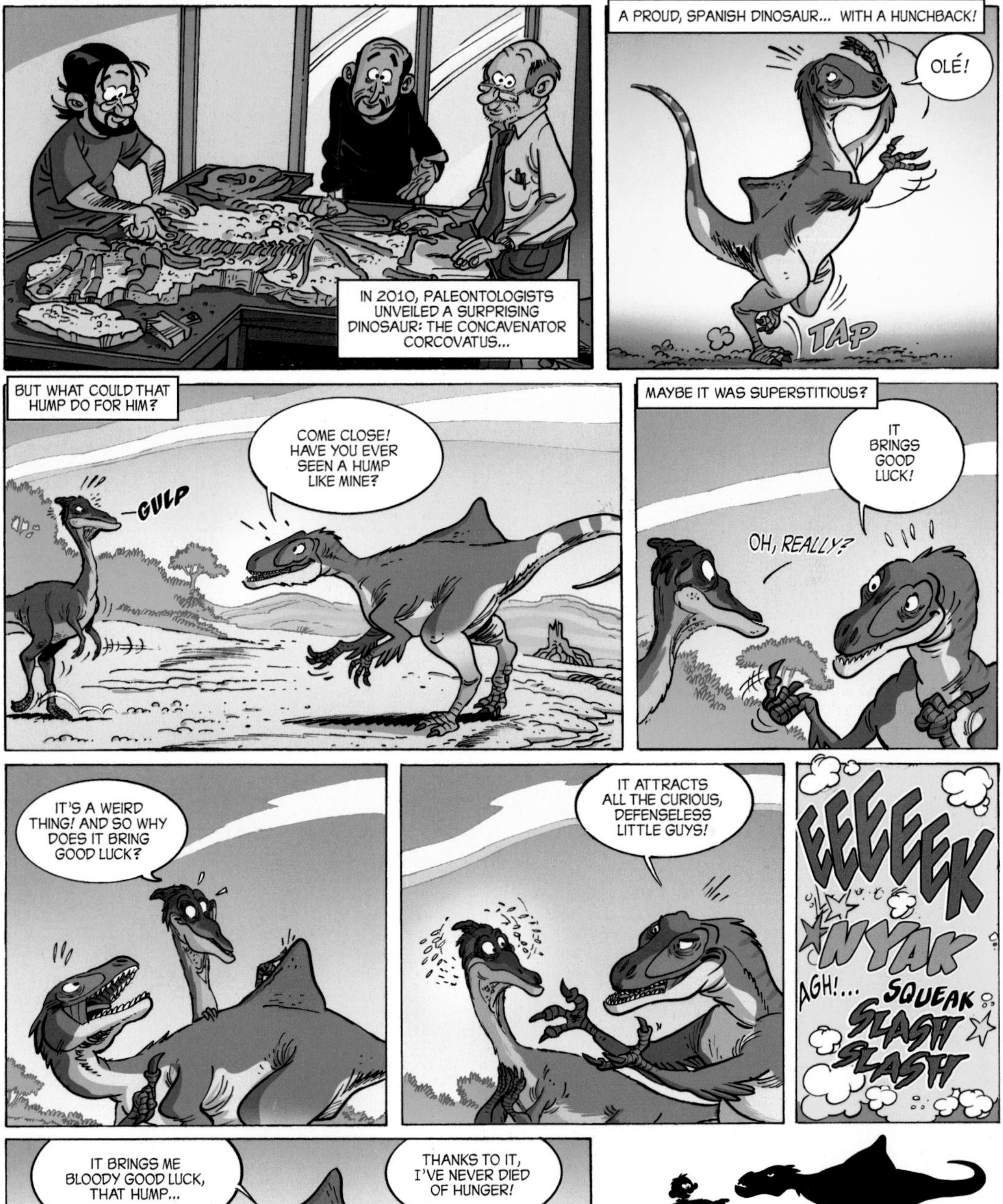
IN 2010, PALEONTOLOGISTS UNVEILED A SURPRISING DINOSAUR: THE CONCAVENATOR CORCOVATUS...
A PROUD, SPANISH DINOSAUR... WITH A HUNCHBACK!
OLÉ!
TAP
BUT WHAT COULD THAT HUMP DO FOR HIM?
GULP
COME CLOSE! HAVE YOU EVER SEEN A HUMP LIKE MINE?
MAYBE IT WAS SUPERSTITIOUS?
IT BRINGS GOOD LUCK!
OH, REALLY?
IT'S A WEIRD THING! AND SO WHY DOES IT BRING GOOD LUCK?
IT ATTRACTS ALL THE CURIOUS, DEFENSELESS LITTLE GUYS!
EEEEEK
NYAK
AGH!...
SQUEAK
SLASH
SLASH

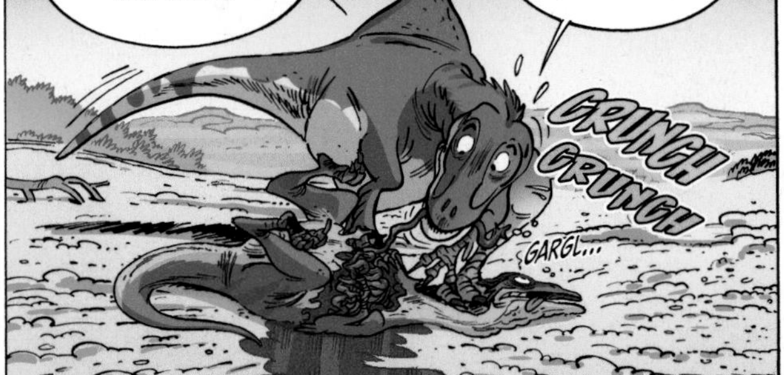
IT BRINGS ME BLOODY GOOD LUCK, THAT HUMP...
THANKS TO IT, I'VE NEVER DIED OF HUNGER!
CRUNCH
CRUNCH
GARGL...

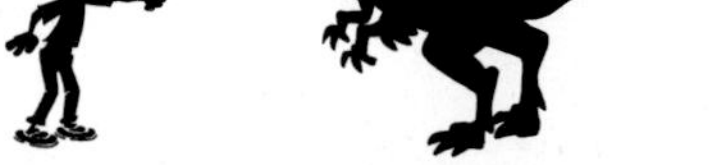

CONCAVENATOR CORCOVATUS

MEANING: HUMPBACKED HUNTER FROM CUENCA
PERIOD: MIDDLE JURASSIC (130 MILLION YEARS AGO)
ORDER/ FAMILY: SAURISCHIA/ CARCHARODONTOSAURIDEA
SIZE: 20 FEET LONG
WEIGHT: 4,400 LBS.
DIET: CARNIVORE
FOUND: SPAIN

PLUMERI & BLOZ

STEGOSAURUS' BRAIN

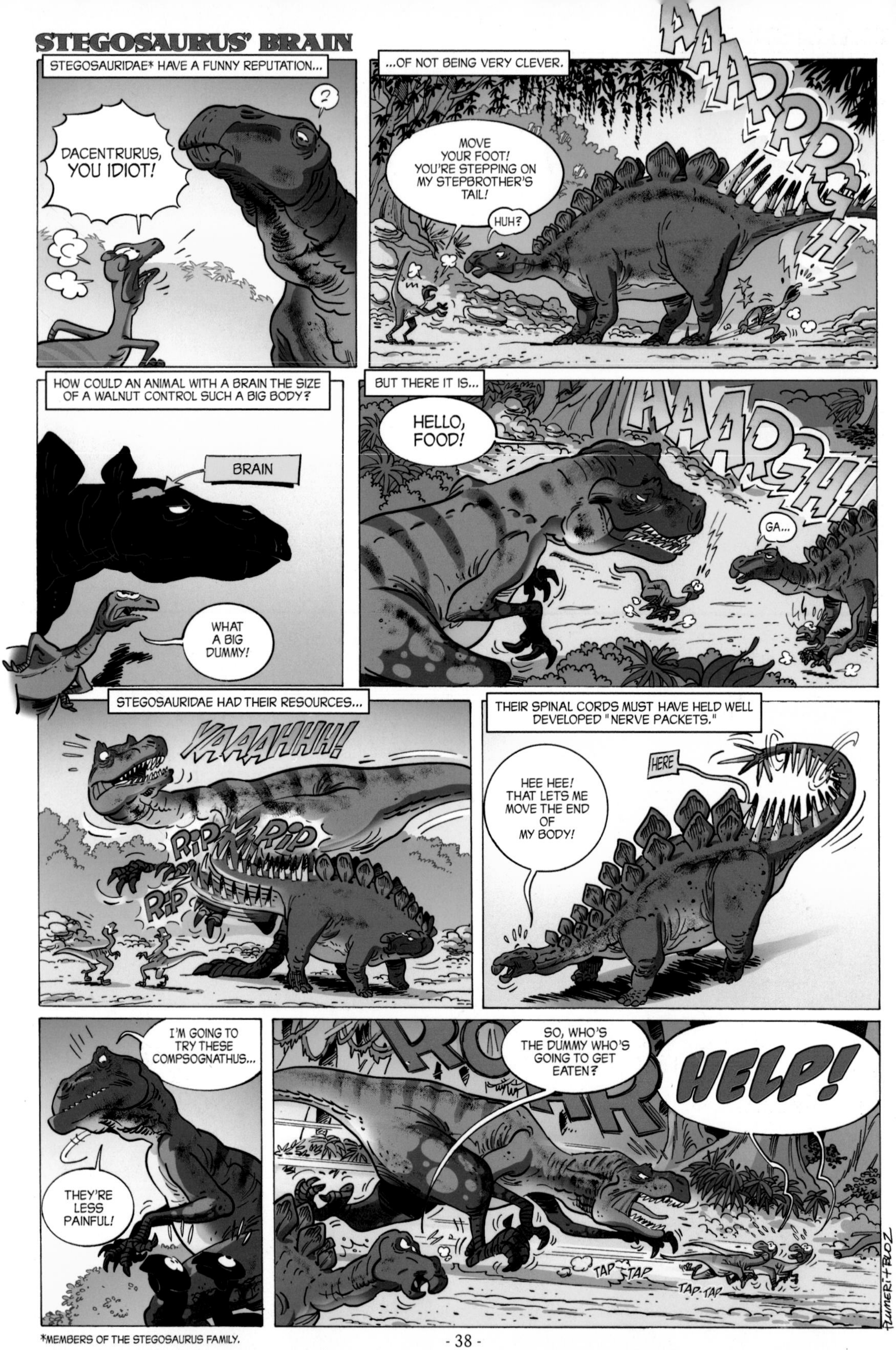
STEGOSAURIDAE* HAVE A FUNNY REPUTATION...
DACENTRURUS, YOU IDIOT!
?
...OF NOT BEING VERY CLEVER.
MOVE YOUR FOOT! YOU'RE STEPPING ON MY STEPBROTHER'S TAIL!
HUH?
AAARRRGH
HOW COULD AN ANIMAL WITH A BRAIN THE SIZE OF A WALNUT CONTROL SUCH A BIG BODY?
BRAIN
WHAT A BIG DUMMY!
BUT THERE IT IS...
HELLO, FOOD!
AAARGH!
GA...
STEGOSAURIDAE HAD THEIR RESOURCES...
YAAAHHH!
RIP RIP
RIP
THEIR SPINAL CORDS MUST HAVE HELD WELL DEVELOPED "NERVE PACKETS."
HERE
HEE HEE! THAT LETS ME MOVE THE END OF MY BODY!
I'M GOING TO TRY THESE COMPSOGNATHUS...
THEY'RE LESS PAINFUL!
ROAR
SO, WHO'S THE DUMMY WHO'S GOING TO GET EATEN?
HELP!
TAP TAP
TAP TAP
PLUMERI + BLOZ

*MEMBERS OF THE STEGOSAURUS FAMILY.

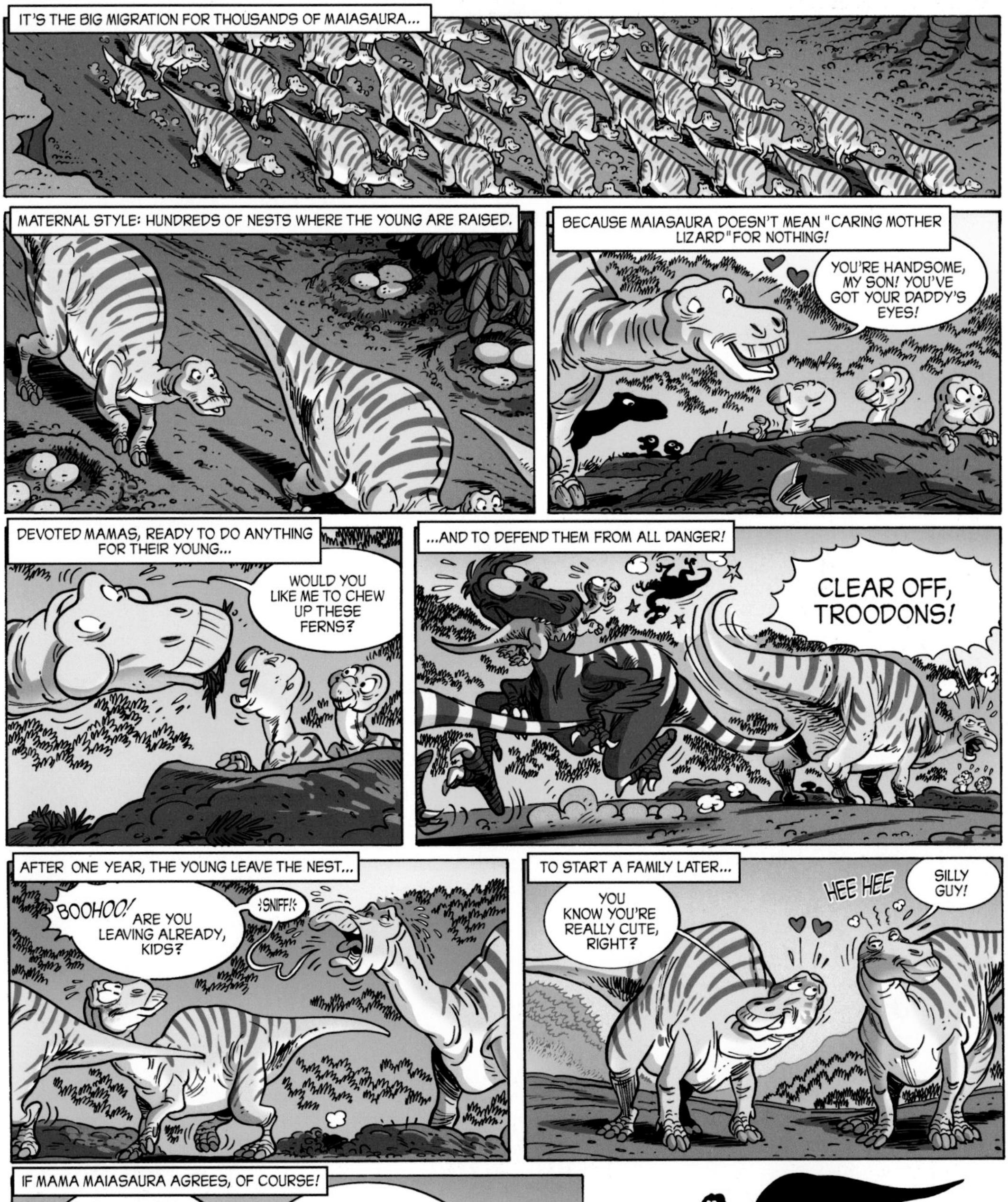
IT'S THE BIG MIGRATION FOR THOUSANDS OF MAIASAURA...
MATERNAL STYLE: HUNDREDS OF NESTS WHERE THE YOUNG ARE RAISED.
BECAUSE MAIASAURA DOESN'T MEAN "CARING MOTHER LIZARD" FOR NOTHING!
YOU'RE HANDSOME, MY SON! YOU'VE GOT YOUR DADDY'S EYES!
DEVOTED MAMAS, READY TO DO ANYTHING FOR THEIR YOUNG...
WOULD YOU LIKE ME TO CHEW UP THESE FERNS?
...AND TO DEFEND THEM FROM ALL DANGER!
CLEAR OFF, TROODONS!
AFTER ONE YEAR, THE YOUNG LEAVE THE NEST...
BOOHOO! ARE YOU LEAVING ALREADY, KIDS?
SNIFF!
TO START A FAMILY LATER...
YOU KNOW YOU'RE REALLY CUTE, RIGHT?
HEE HEE
SILLY GUY!

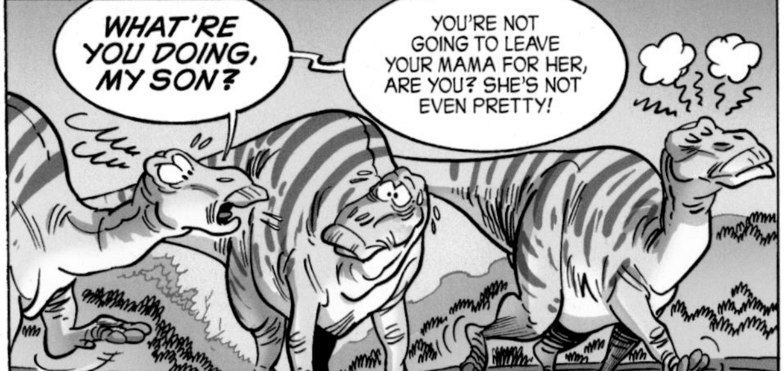
IF MAMA MAIASAURA AGREES, OF COURSE!
WHAT'RE YOU DOING, MY SON?
YOU'RE NOT GOING TO LEAVE YOUR MAMA FOR HER, ARE YOU? SHE'S NOT EVEN PRETTY!

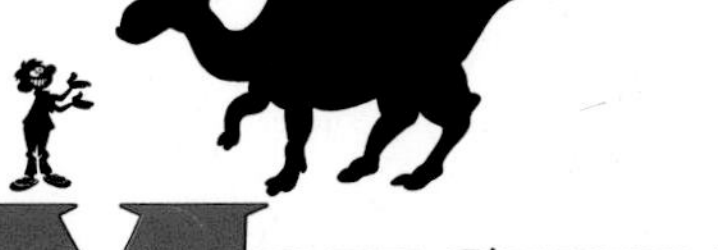

MAIASAURA

MEANING: CARING MOTHER LIZARD
PERIOD: LATE CRETACEOUS (80-72 MILLION YEARS AGO)
ORDER/ FAMILY: ORNITHISCHIA/HADROSAURIDAE
SIZE: 30 FEET LONG
WEIGHT: 6,600 POUNDS
DIET: HERBIVORE
FOUND: NORTH AMERICA

PLUMERI & BLOZ

COMPSOGNATHUS HUNTERS (2)

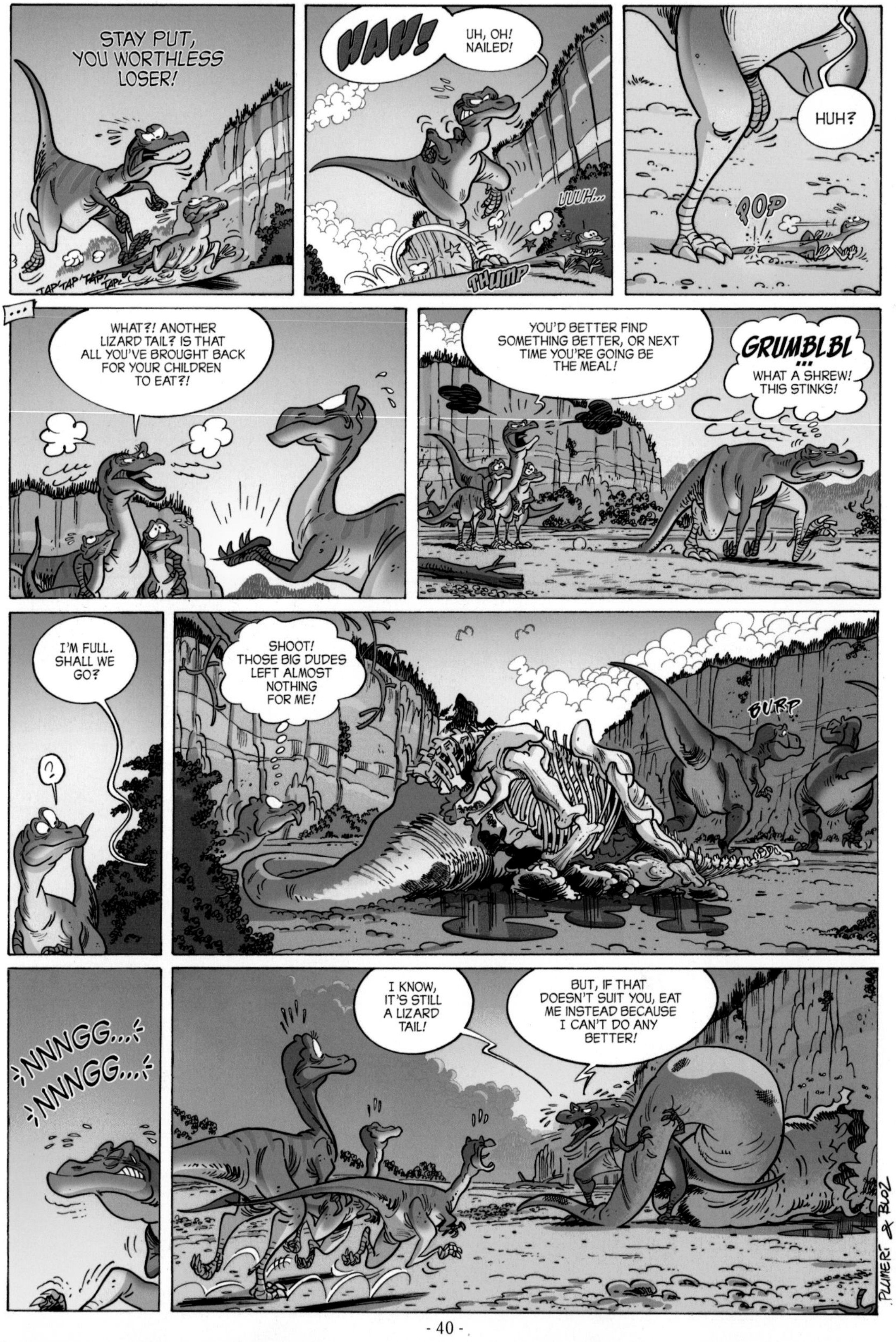
STAY PUT, YOU WORTHLESS LOSER!
TAP TAP TAP TAP
HAH!
UH, OH! NAILED!
UUUH...
THUMP
HUH?
POP
WHAT?! ANOTHER LIZARD TAIL? IS THAT ALL YOU'VE BROUGHT BACK FOR YOUR CHILDREN TO EAT?!
YOU'D BETTER FIND SOMETHING BETTER, OR NEXT TIME YOU'RE GOING BE THE MEAL!
GRUMBLBL
WHAT A SHREW! THIS STINKS!
I'M FULL. SHALL WE GO?
?
SHOOT! THOSE BIG DUDES LEFT ALMOST NOTHING FOR ME!
BURP
NNNGG...
NNNGG...
I KNOW, IT'S STILL A LIZARD TAIL!
BUT, IF THAT DOESN'T SUIT YOU, EAT ME INSTEAD BECAUSE I CAN'T DO ANY BETTER!
PLUMERI & BLOZ

DILOPHOSAURUS

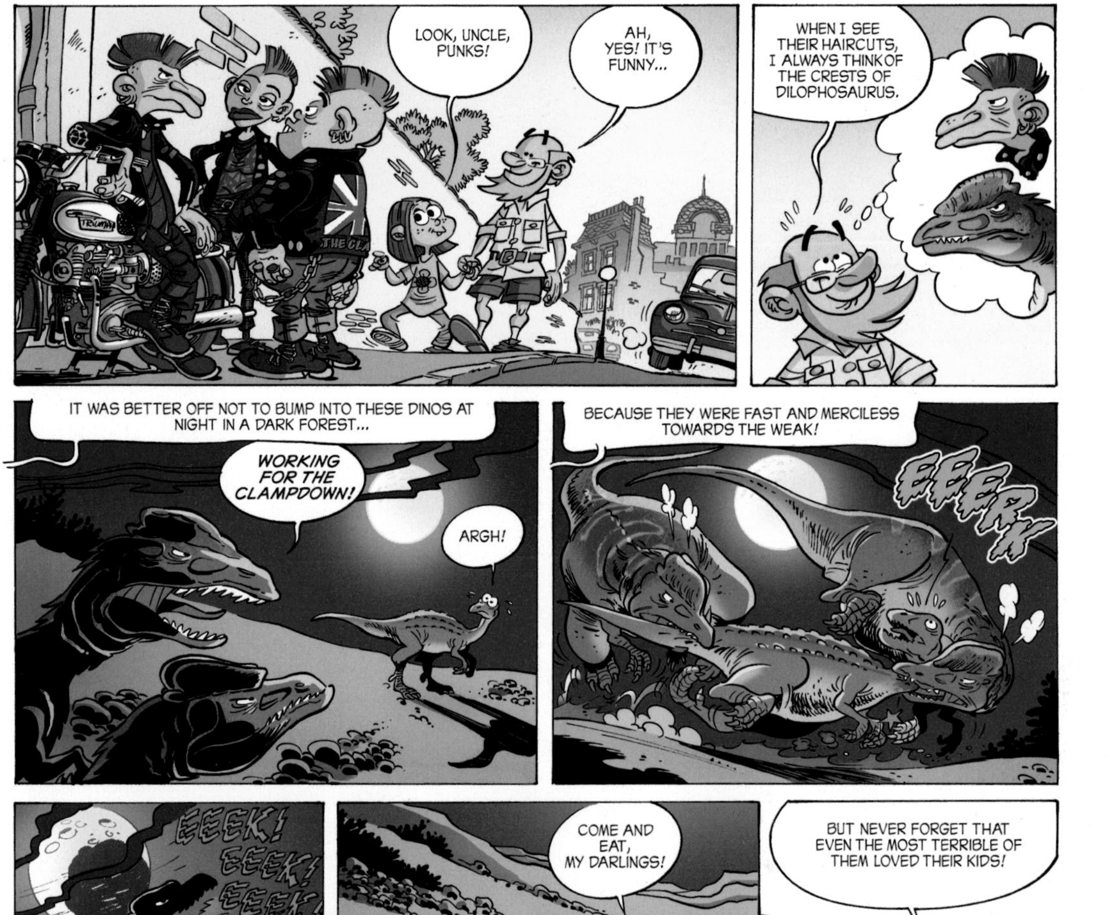

LOOK, UNCLE, PUNKS!
AH, YES! IT'S FUNNY...
WHEN I SEE THEIR HAIRCUTS, I ALWAYS THINK OF THE CRESTS OF DILOPHOSAURUS.
IT WAS BETTER OFF NOT TO BUMP INTO THESE DINOS AT NIGHT IN A DARK FOREST...
WORKING FOR THE CLAMPDOWN!
ARGH!
BECAUSE THEY WERE FAST AND MERCILESS TOWARDS THE WEAK!
EEERK
EEEK! EEEK! EEEK!
COME AND EAT, MY DARLINGS!
BUT NEVER FORGET THAT EVEN THE MOST TERRIBLE OF THEM LOVED THEIR KIDS!

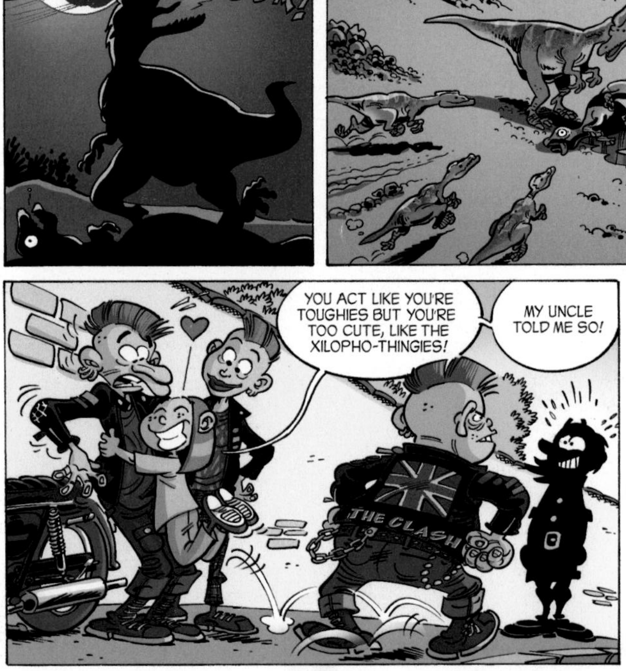

YOU ACT LIKE YOU'RE TOUGHIES BUT YOU'RE TOO CUTE, LIKE THE XILOPHO-THINGIES!
MY UNCLE TOLD ME SO!
THE CLASH

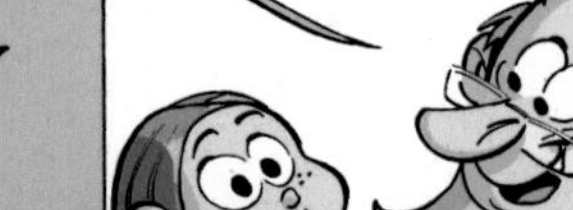

DILOPHOSAURUS

MEANING: TWO-CRESTED LIZARD
PERIOD: EARLY JURASSIC (200-189 MILLION YEARS AGO)
ORDER/ FAMILY: SAURISCHIA/ DILOPHOSAURIDAE
SIZE: 20 FEET LONG
WEIGHT: 1,100 LBS.
DIET: CARNIVORE
FOUND: NORTH AMERICA, CHINA

PLUMERITRUC & BLOZMACHIN.

BIZARRE RECORDS

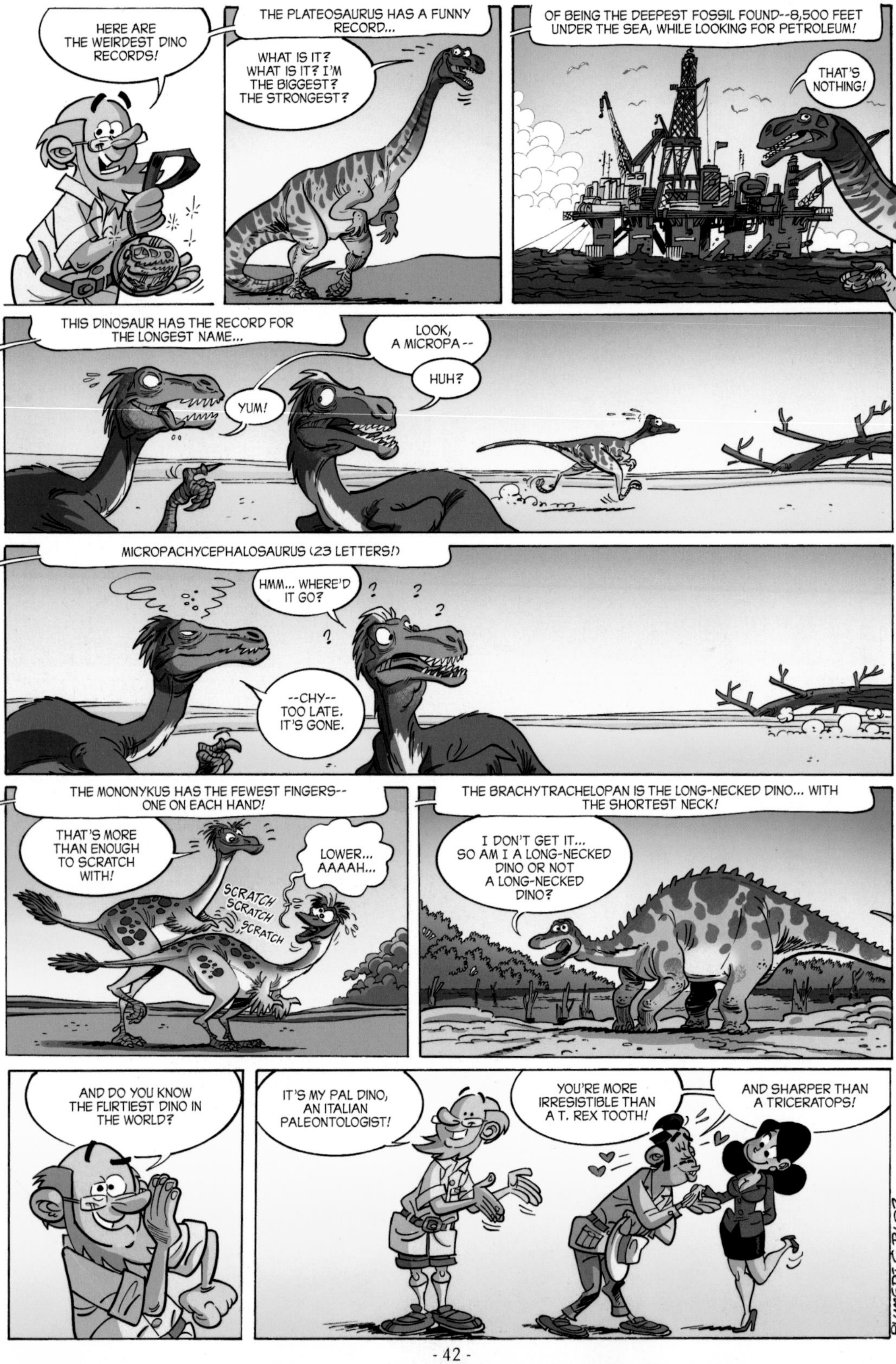

HERE ARE THE WEIRDEST DINO RECORDS!
THE PLATEOSAURUS HAS A FUNNY RECORD...
WHAT IS IT? WHAT IS IT? I'M THE BIGGEST? THE STRONGEST?
OF BEING THE DEEPEST FOSSIL FOUND--8,500 FEET UNDER THE SEA, WHILE LOOKING FOR PETROLEUM!
THAT'S NOTHING!
THIS DINOSAUR HAS THE RECORD FOR THE LONGEST NAME...
LOOK, A MICROPA--
HUH?
YUM!
MICROPACHYCEPHALOSAURUS (23 LETTERS!)
HMM... WHERE'D IT GO?
--CHY-- TOO LATE. IT'S GONE.
THE MONONYKUS HAS THE FEWEST FINGERS-- ONE ON EACH HAND!
THAT'S MORE THAN ENOUGH TO SCRATCH WITH!
LOWER... AAAAH...
SCRATCH SCRATCH SCRATCH
THE BRACHYTRACHELOPAN IS THE LONG-NECKED DINO... WITH THE SHORTEST NECK!
I DON'T GET IT... SO AM I A LONG-NECKED DINO OR NOT A LONG-NECKED DINO?
AND DO YOU KNOW THE FLIRTIEST DINO IN THE WORLD?
IT'S MY PAL DINO, AN ITALIAN PALEONTOLOGIST!
YOU'RE MORE IRRESISTIBLE THAN A T. REX TOOTH!
AND SHARPER THAN A TRICERATOPS!
PLUMERI & BLOZ

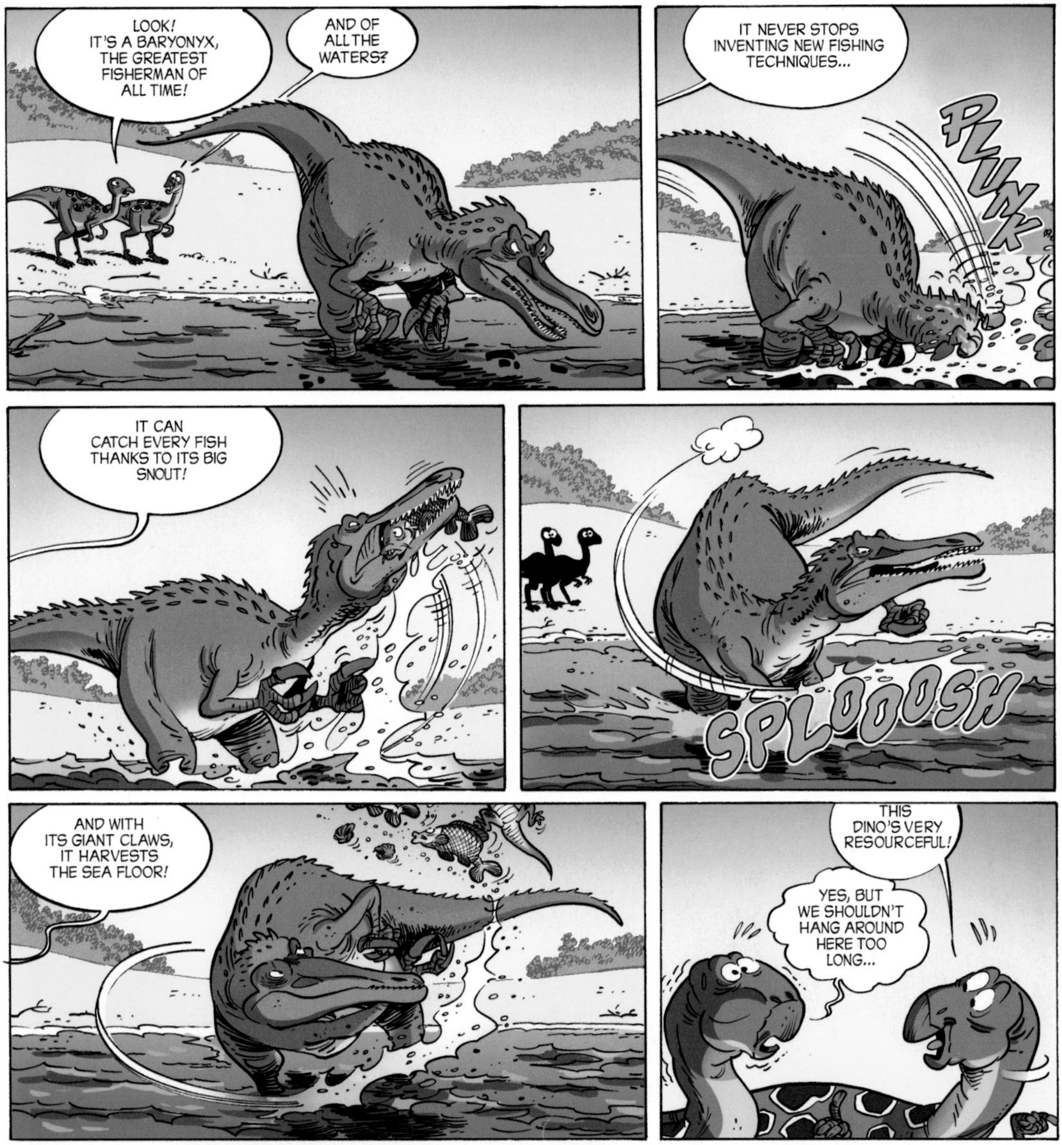
LOOK! IT'S A BARYONYX, THE GREATEST FISHERMAN OF ALL TIME!
AND OF ALL THE WATERS?
IT NEVER STOPS INVENTING NEW FISHING TECHNIQUES...
PLUNK
IT CAN CATCH EVERY FISH THANKS TO ITS BIG SNOUT!
SPLOOOSH
AND WITH ITS GIANT CLAWS, IT HARVESTS THE SEA FLOOR!
THIS DINO'S VERY RESOURCEFUL!
YES, BUT WE SHOULDN'T HANG AROUND HERE TOO LONG...

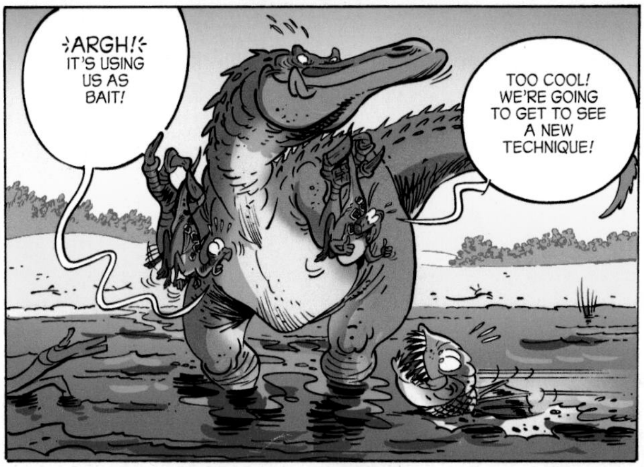
ARGH! IT'S USING US AS BAIT!
TOO COOL! WE'RE GOING TO GET TO SEE A NEW TECHNIQUE!

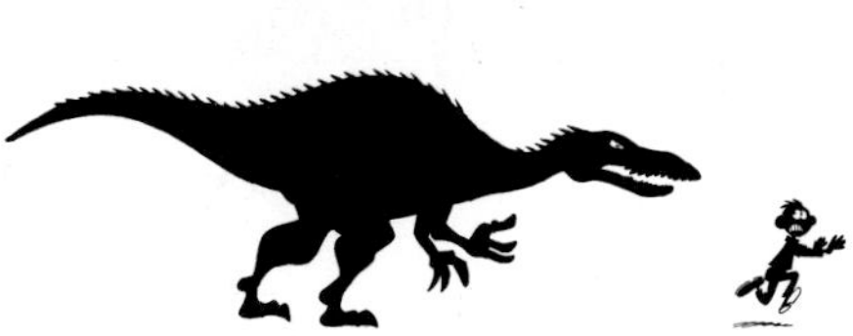

BARYONYX

MEANING: HEAVY CLAW
PERIOD: EARLY CRETACEOUS (140-112 MILLION YEARS AGO)
ORDER/ FAMILY: SAURISCHIA/ SPINOSAURIDAE
SIZE: 33 FEET LONG
WEIGHT: 4,500 LBS.
DIET: PISCIVORE AND CARNIVORE
FOUND: ENGLAND, SPAIN, AND PORTUGAL

PLUMERI & BLOZ

THE STRANGE DEINOCHEIRUS

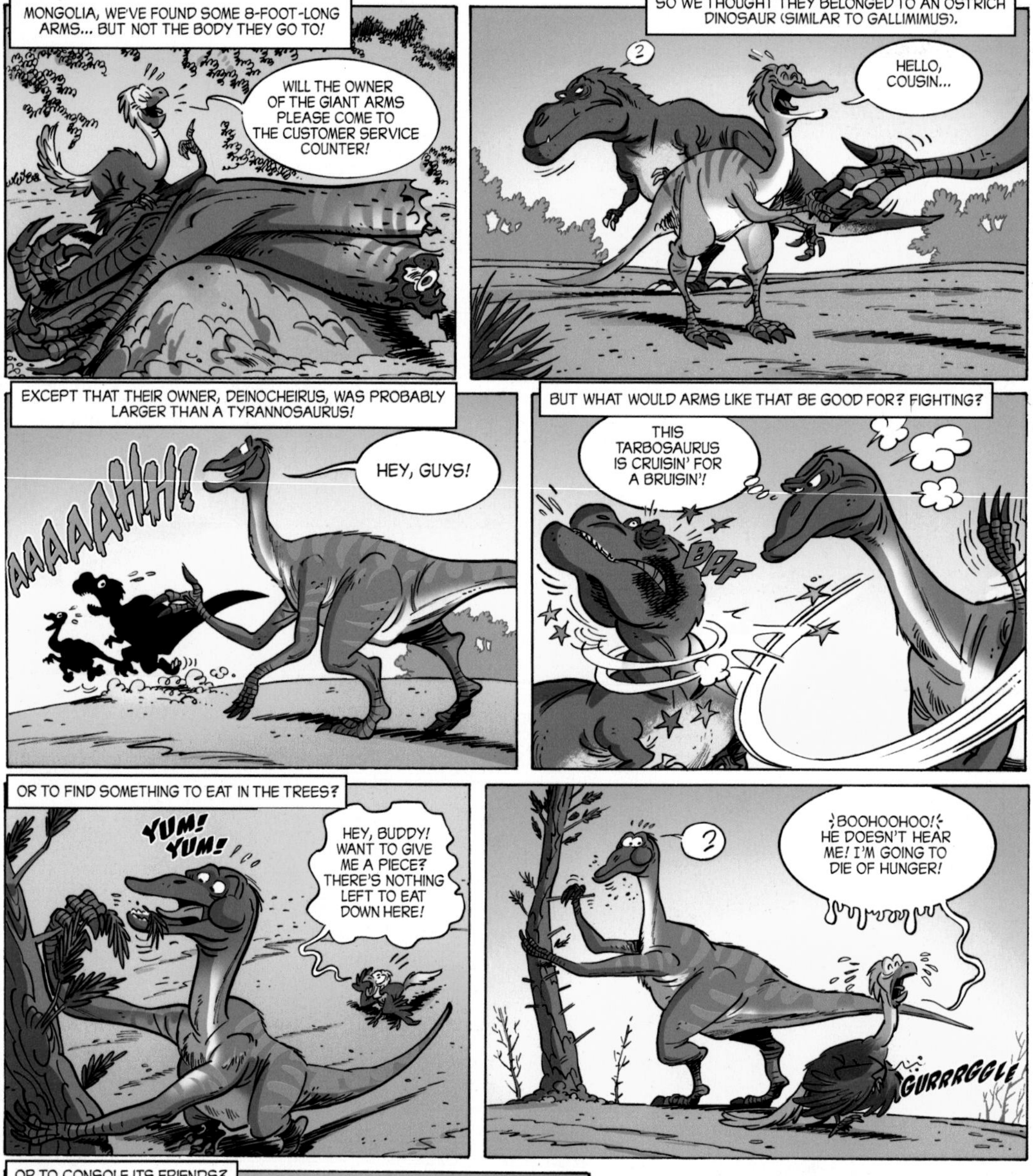
MONGOLIA, WE'VE FOUND SOME 8-FOOT-LONG ARMS... BUT NOT THE BODY THEY GO TO!
WILL THE OWNER OF THE GIANT ARMS PLEASE COME TO THE CUSTOMER SERVICE COUNTER!
SO WE THOUGHT THEY BELONGED TO AN OSTRICH DINOSAUR (SIMILAR TO GALLIMIMUS).
?
HELLO, COUSIN...
EXCEPT THAT THEIR OWNER, DEINOCHEIRUS, WAS PROBABLY LARGER THAN A TYRANNOSAURUS!
AAAAAHHH!
HEY, GUYS!
BUT WHAT WOULD ARMS LIKE THAT BE GOOD FOR? FIGHTING?
THIS TARBOSAURUS IS CRUISIN' FOR A BRUISIN'!
BAF
OR TO FIND SOMETHING TO EAT IN THE TREES?
YUM! YUM!
HEY, BUDDY! WANT TO GIVE ME A PIECE? THERE'S NOTHING LEFT TO EAT DOWN HERE!
?
BOOHOOHOO! HE DOESN'T HEAR ME! I'M GOING TO DIE OF HUNGER!
GURRRGGLE

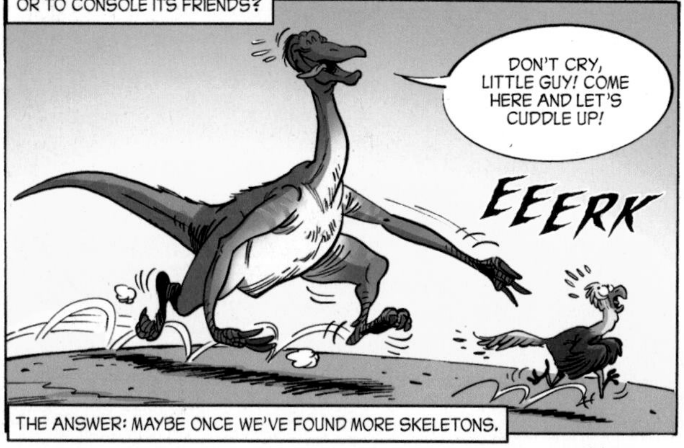
OR TO CONSOLE ITS FRIENDS?
DON'T CRY, LITTLE GUY! COME HERE AND LET'S CUDDLE UP!
EEERK
THE ANSWER: MAYBE ONCE WE'VE FOUND MORE SKELETONS.

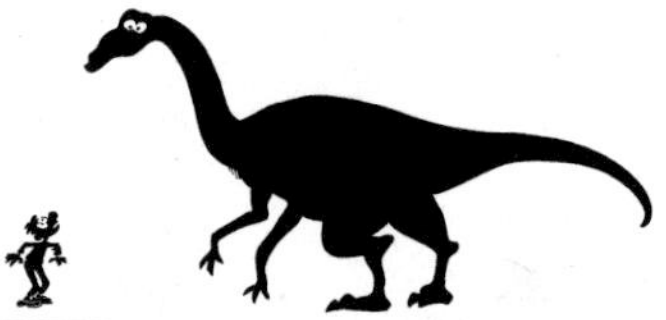

DEINOCHEIRUS

MEANING: TERRIBLE HAND
PERIOD: LATE CRETACEOUS (70 MILLION YEARS AGO)
ORDER/ FAMILY: SAURISCHIA/ DEINOCHEIRIDAE
SIZE: 35-50 FEET LONG?
WEIGHT: 4,400-11,000 LBS.?
DIET: HERBIVORE OR OMNIVORE?
FOUND: MONGOLIA

PLUMERI & BLOZ

CERATOPSIAN COMPETITION

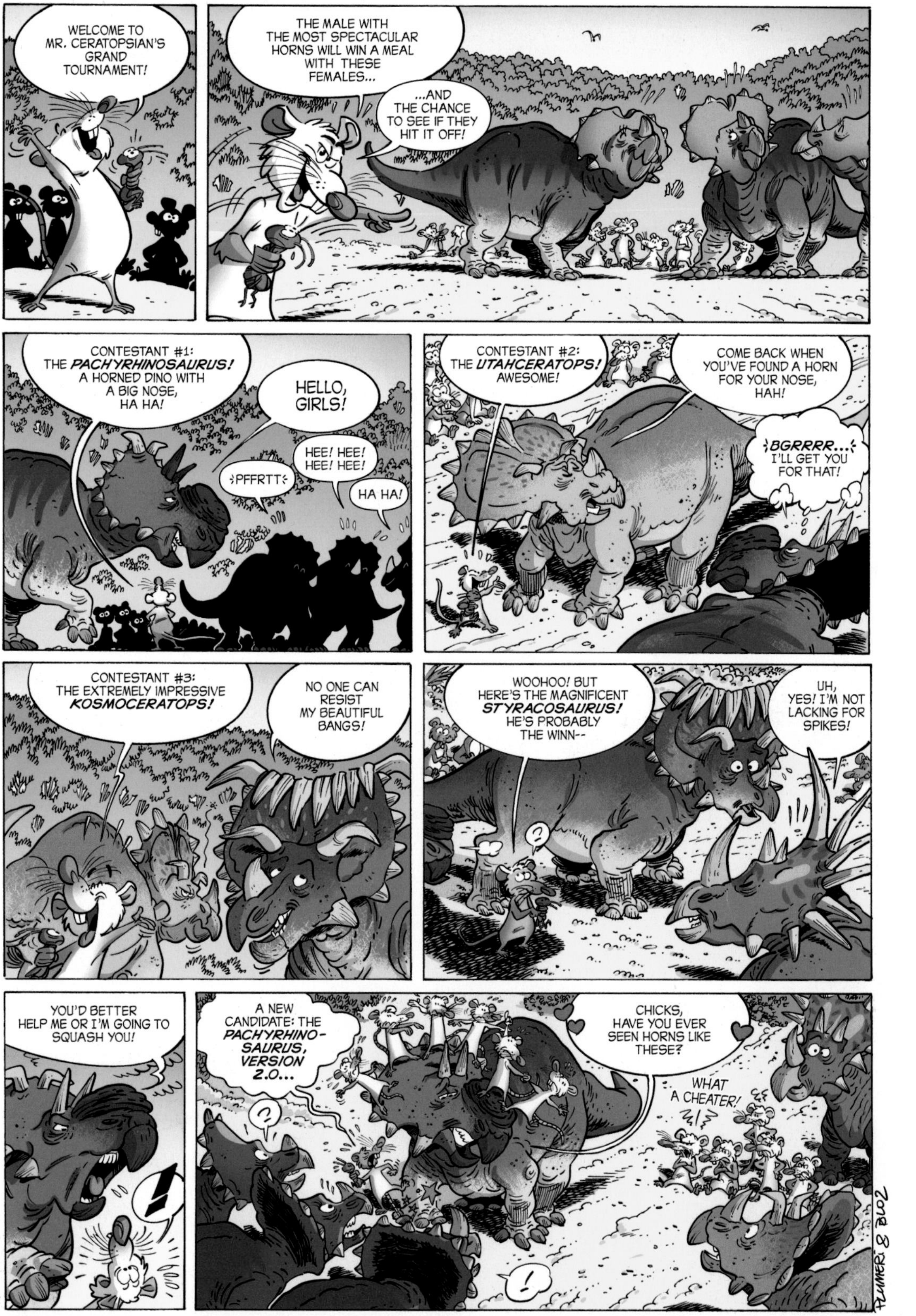
WELCOME TO MR. CERATOPSIAN'S GRAND TOURNAMENT!
THE MALE WITH THE MOST SPECTACULAR HORNS WILL WIN A MEAL WITH THESE FEMALES...
...AND THE CHANCE TO SEE IF THEY HIT IT OFF!
CONTESTANT #1: THE PACHYRHINOSAURUS! A HORNED DINO WITH A BIG NOSE, HA HA!
HELLO, GIRLS!
PFFRTT
HEE! HEE! HEE! HEE!
HA HA!
CONTESTANT #2: THE UTAHCERATOPS! AWESOME!
COME BACK WHEN YOU'VE FOUND A HORN FOR YOUR NOSE, HAH!
BGRRRR... I'LL GET YOU FOR THAT!
CONTESTANT #3: THE EXTREMELY IMPRESSIVE KOSMOCERATOPS!
NO ONE CAN RESIST MY BEAUTIFUL BANGS!
WOOHOO! BUT HERE'S THE MAGNIFICENT STYRACOSAURUS! HE'S PROBABLY THE WINN--
UH, YES! I'M NOT LACKING FOR SPIKES!
?
YOU'D BETTER HELP ME OR I'M GOING TO SQUASH YOU!
!
A NEW CANDIDATE: THE PACHYRHINO-SAURUS, VERSION 2.0...
?
CHICKS, HAVE YOU EVER SEEN HORNS LIKE THESE?
WHAT A CHEATER!
!
!
PLUMERI & BLOZ

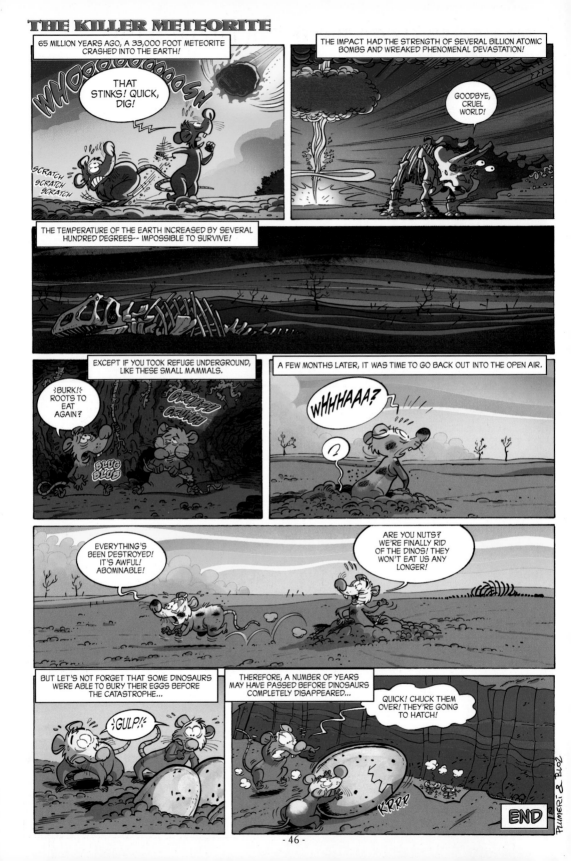

THE KILLER METEORITE

65 MILLION YEARS AGO, A 33,000 FOOT METEORITE CRASHED INTO THE EARTH!

WHOoooooooSH

THAT STINKS! QUICK, DIG!

SCRATCH SCRATCH SCRATCH

THE IMPACT HAD THE STRENGTH OF SEVERAL BILLION ATOMIC BOMBS AND WREAKED PHENOMENAL DEVASTATION!

GOODBYE, CRUEL WORLD!

THE TEMPERATURE OF THE EARTH INCREASED BY SEVERAL HUNDRED DEGREES-- IMPOSSIBLE TO SURVIVE!

EXCEPT IF YOU TOOK REFUGE UNDERGROUND, LIKE THESE SMALL MAMMALS.

‡BURK!‡ ROOTS TO EAT AGAIN?

GROMPH GROMPH

BLUG BLUG

A FEW MONTHS LATER, IT WAS TIME TO GO BACK OUT INTO THE OPEN AIR.

WHHHAAA?

?

EVERYTHING'S BEEN DESTROYED! IT'S AWFUL! ABOMINABLE!

ARE YOU NUTS? WE'RE FINALLY RID OF THE DINOS! THEY WON'T EAT US ANY LONGER!

BUT LET'S NOT FORGET THAT SOME DINOSAURS WERE ABLE TO BURY THEIR EGGS BEFORE THE CATASTROPHE...

‡GULP!‡

THEREFORE, A NUMBER OF YEARS MAY HAVE PASSED BEFORE DINOSAURS COMPLETELY DISAPPEARED...

QUICK! CHUCK THEM OVER! THEY'RE GOING TO HATCH!

KRRR

END

PLUMERI & BLOZ

WATCH OUT FOR PAPERCUTZ™

Welcome to the savage second DINOSAURS graphic novel by Arnaud Plumeri and Bloz from Papercutz, the prehistoric people dedicated to publishing great graphic novels for all ages! I'm Jim Salicrup, the Editor-in-Chief That Walks Like a Man, here to fill you in on a few fun facts pertaining to Papercutz—the first being that you should definitely check out our wonderful website– papercutz.com– for all the latest news and previews on DINOSAURS and all our other awesome graphic novels.

But let's pause a moment to reflect on DINOSAURS #1 "In the Beginning…" We're happy to report that it appears our premiere DINOSAURS publication has been warmly greeted by teachers, librarians, parents, and Dino-lovers of all ages. The reviews have been very positive, and sales seem to be strong. This makes us very happy because, as with all Papercutz graphic novels, we're publishing material that we love and hope that you will enjoy it as much as we do!

Speaking of which, we just received this lovely email from DINOSAURS author Arnaud Plumeri and thought we'd share it with you…

> "I've just got DINOSAURS #1 'In the Beginning' and I think you could use a warm thank you from the authors! You did quality work and I hope you will be satisfied with the results. DINOSAURS are now in good (and tiny) hands! (Meet my twins).

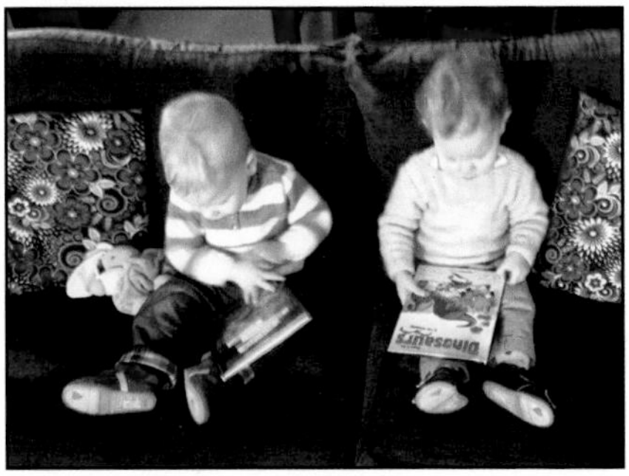

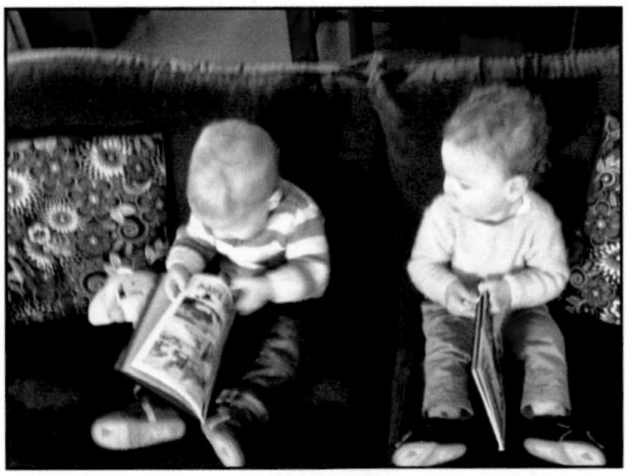

Thanks,

Arnaud Plumeri."

Mr. Plumeri is way too kind! After all, he and Bloz did all the creative work, writing and drawing DINOSAURS, in the first place. Our part was relatively easy—simply assembling it all and getting it to YOU! And as a Gemini, I got a special kick out of seeing the Plumeri twins looking over DINOSAURS #1.

If the twins want even more comics with dinosaurs, I hope they take my advice from DINOSAURS #1 and check out such Papercutz graphic novels as MONSTER #3 "MONSTER DINOSAUR" or GERONIMO STILTON #7 "Dinosaurs in Action." I'll even add GERONIMO STILTON #5 "The Great Ice Age"!

But, if they're looking for a fun change of pace, may I suggest THE GARFIELD SHOW? Featuring the very same lasagna-loving fat cat as you see starring in his very own Cartoon Network TV series, each volume is packed with fun stories that take you places such as the Land of the Cat People! To give you just a small taste of what you'll find in THE GARFIELD SHOW #3 "Long Lost Lyman," we're offering a special preview on the following pages. No need to thank us! We enjoy sharing what we love with friends such as you!

And don't forget about DINOSAURS #3 "Jurassic Smarts" coming soon—filled with more Dino-facts and fun than you can shake an Allosaurus at!

Thanks,

JIM

Salicrupsaurus (Page 47)
Meaning: Big-Headed Editor
Period: Silver Age to Modern Age (57 Years Ago)
Order/ Family: Geekasaurs/ Salicrupidae
Size: 6'2"
Weight: 250 lbs.?
Diet: Omnivore
Found: North America (If found, return to Papercutz)

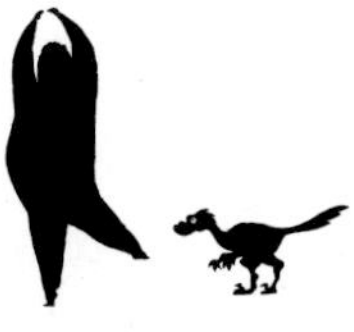

STAY IN TOUCH!

EMAIL: salicrup@papercutz.com
WEB: www.papercutz.com
TWITTER: @papercutzgn
FACEBOOK: PAPERCUTZGRAPHICNOVELS
MAIL: Papercutz, 160 Broadway, Suite 700, East Wing, New York, NY 10038

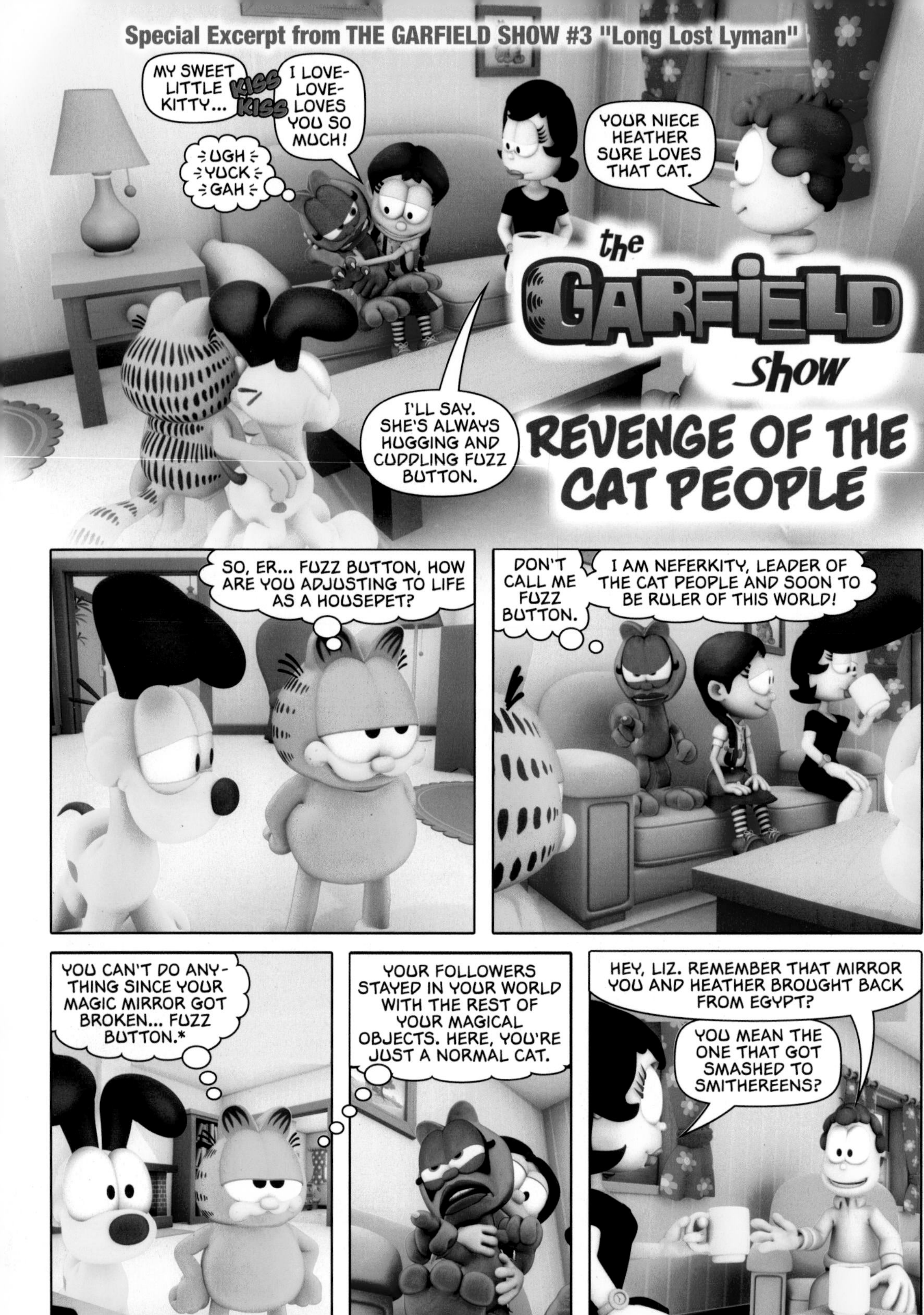

Special Excerpt from THE GARFIELD SHOW #3 "Long Lost Lyman"
MY SWEET LITTLE KITTY...
KISS KISS
I LOVE-LOVE-LOVES YOU SO MUCH!
UGH YUCK GAH
YOUR NIECE HEATHER SURE LOVES THAT CAT.
I'LL SAY. SHE'S ALWAYS HUGGING AND CUDDLING FUZZ BUTTON.
the GARFIELD show
REVENGE OF THE CAT PEOPLE
SO, ER... FUZZ BUTTON, HOW ARE YOU ADJUSTING TO LIFE AS A HOUSEPET?
DON'T CALL ME FUZZ BUTTON.
I AM NEFERKITY, LEADER OF THE CAT PEOPLE AND SOON TO BE RULER OF THIS WORLD!
YOU CAN'T DO ANYTHING SINCE YOUR MAGIC MIRROR GOT BROKEN... FUZZ BUTTON.*
YOUR FOLLOWERS STAYED IN YOUR WORLD WITH THE REST OF YOUR MAGICAL OBJECTS. HERE, YOU'RE JUST A NORMAL CAT.
HEY, LIZ. REMEMBER THAT MIRROR YOU AND HEATHER BROUGHT BACK FROM EGYPT?
YOU MEAN THE ONE THAT GOT SMASHED TO SMITHEREENS?

* IF YOU DON'T KNOW WHAT THIS MEANS, YOU MISSED **GARFIELD** & CO #2 "THE CURSE OF THE CAT PEOPLE." DON'T LET THAT HAPPEN AGAIN.

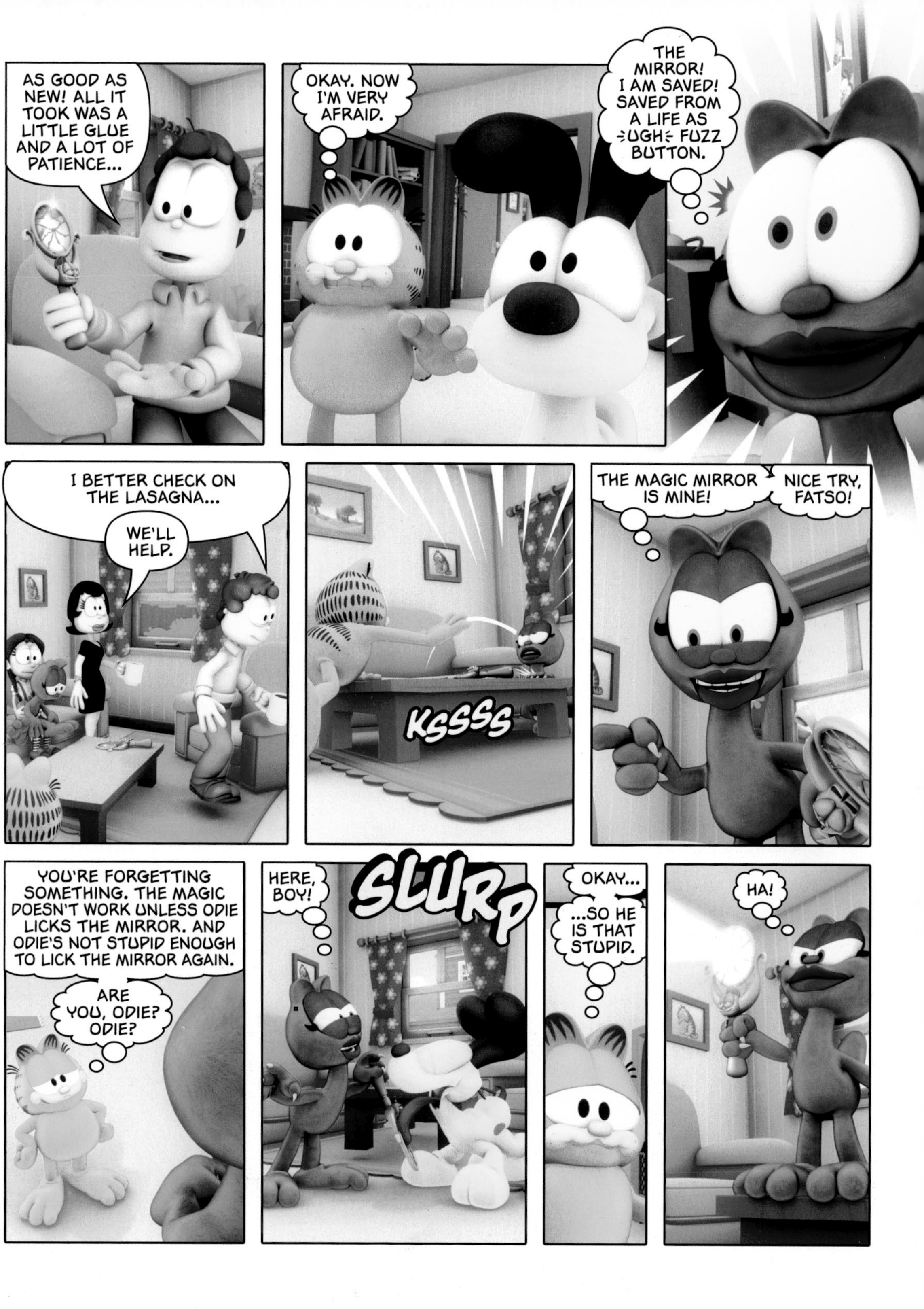
AS GOOD AS NEW! ALL IT TOOK WAS A LITTLE GLUE AND A LOT OF PATIENCE...
OKAY. NOW I'M VERY AFRAID.
THE MIRROR! I AM SAVED! SAVED FROM A LIFE AS =UGH= FUZZ BUTTON.
I BETTER CHECK ON THE LASAGNA...
WE'LL HELP.
KSSSS
THE MAGIC MIRROR IS MINE!
NICE TRY, FATSO!
YOU'RE FORGETTING SOMETHING. THE MAGIC DOESN'T WORK UNLESS ODIE LICKS THE MIRROR. AND ODIE'S NOT STUPID ENOUGH TO LICK THE MIRROR AGAIN.
ARE YOU, ODIE? ODIE?
HERE, BOY!
SLURP
OKAY...
...SO HE IS THAT STUPID.
HA!

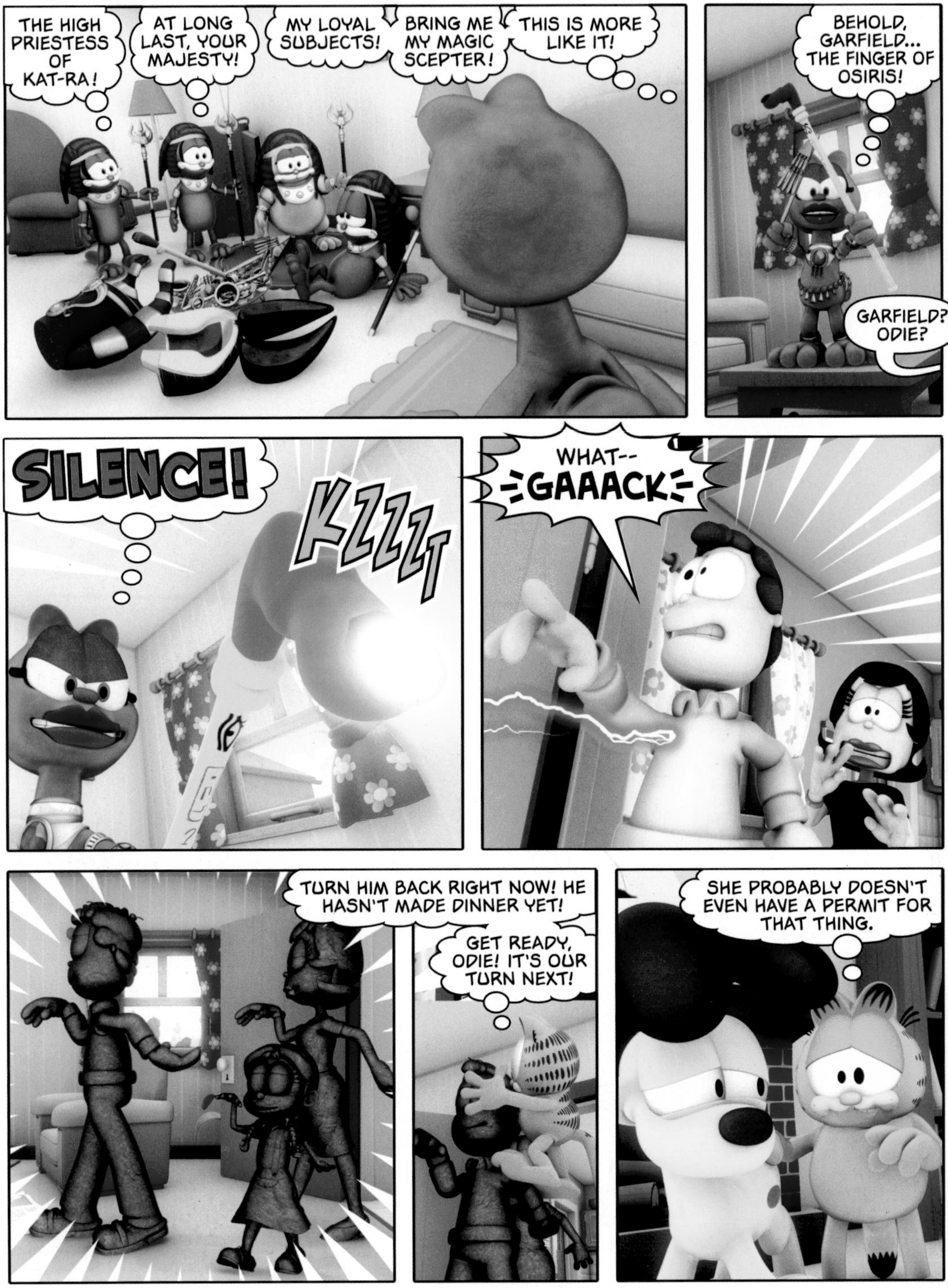

THE HIGH PRIESTESS OF KAT-RA!
AT LONG LAST, YOUR MAJESTY!
MY LOYAL SUBJECTS!
BRING ME MY MAGIC SCEPTER!
THIS IS MORE LIKE IT!
BEHOLD, GARFIELD... THE FINGER OF OSIRIS!
GARFIELD? ODIE?
SILENCE!
KZZZT
WHAT-- GAAACK
TURN HIM BACK RIGHT NOW! HE HASN'T MADE DINNER YET!
GET READY, ODIE! IT'S OUR TURN NEXT!
SHE PROBABLY DOESN'T EVEN HAVE A PERMIT FOR THAT THING.

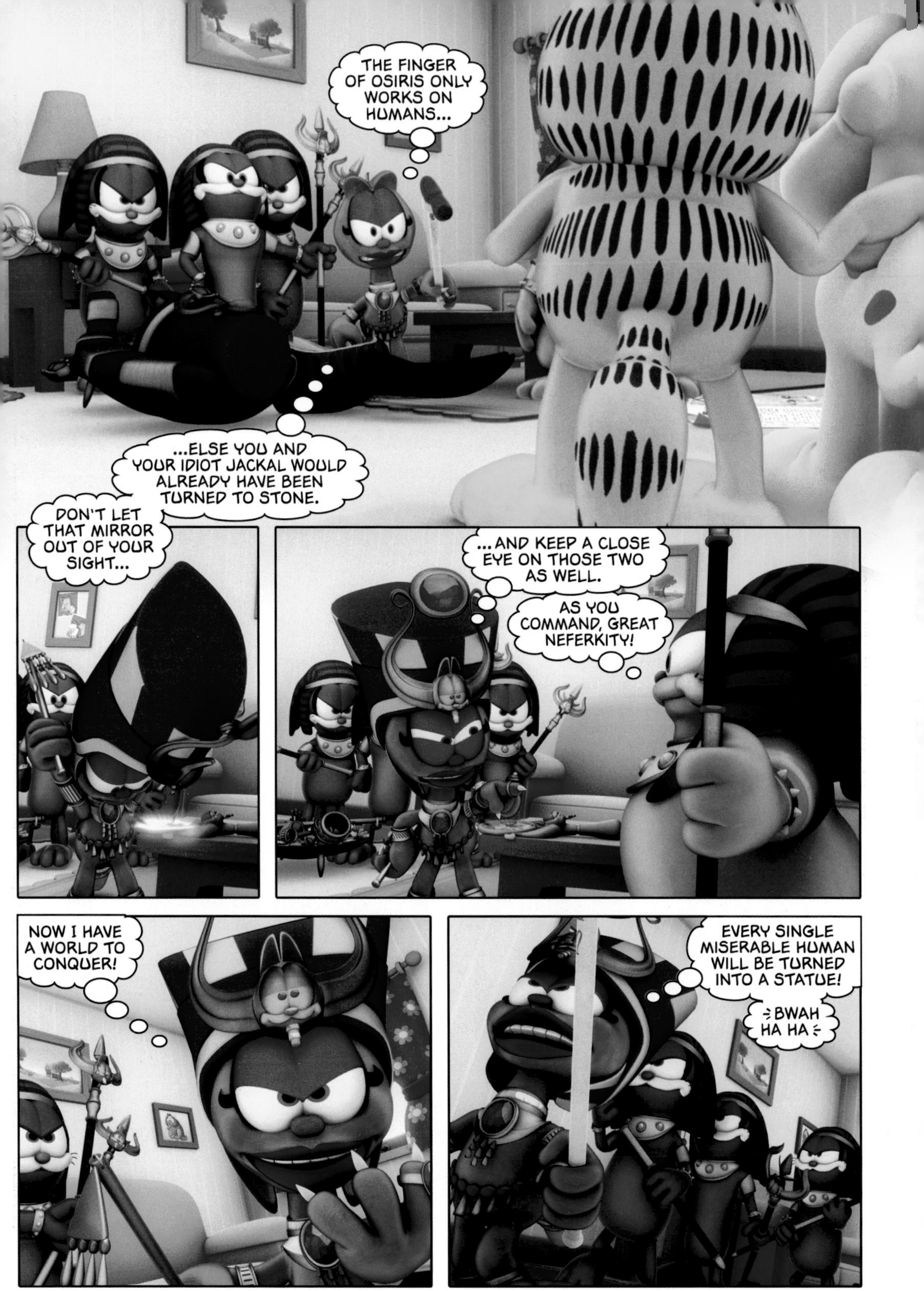
THE FINGER OF OSIRIS ONLY WORKS ON HUMANS...
...ELSE YOU AND YOUR IDIOT JACKAL WOULD ALREADY HAVE BEEN TURNED TO STONE.
DON'T LET THAT MIRROR OUT OF YOUR SIGHT...
...AND KEEP A CLOSE EYE ON THOSE TWO AS WELL.
AS YOU COMMAND, GREAT NEFERKITY!
NOW I HAVE A WORLD TO CONQUER!
EVERY SINGLE MISERABLE HUMAN WILL BE TURNED INTO A STATUE!
BWAH HA HA

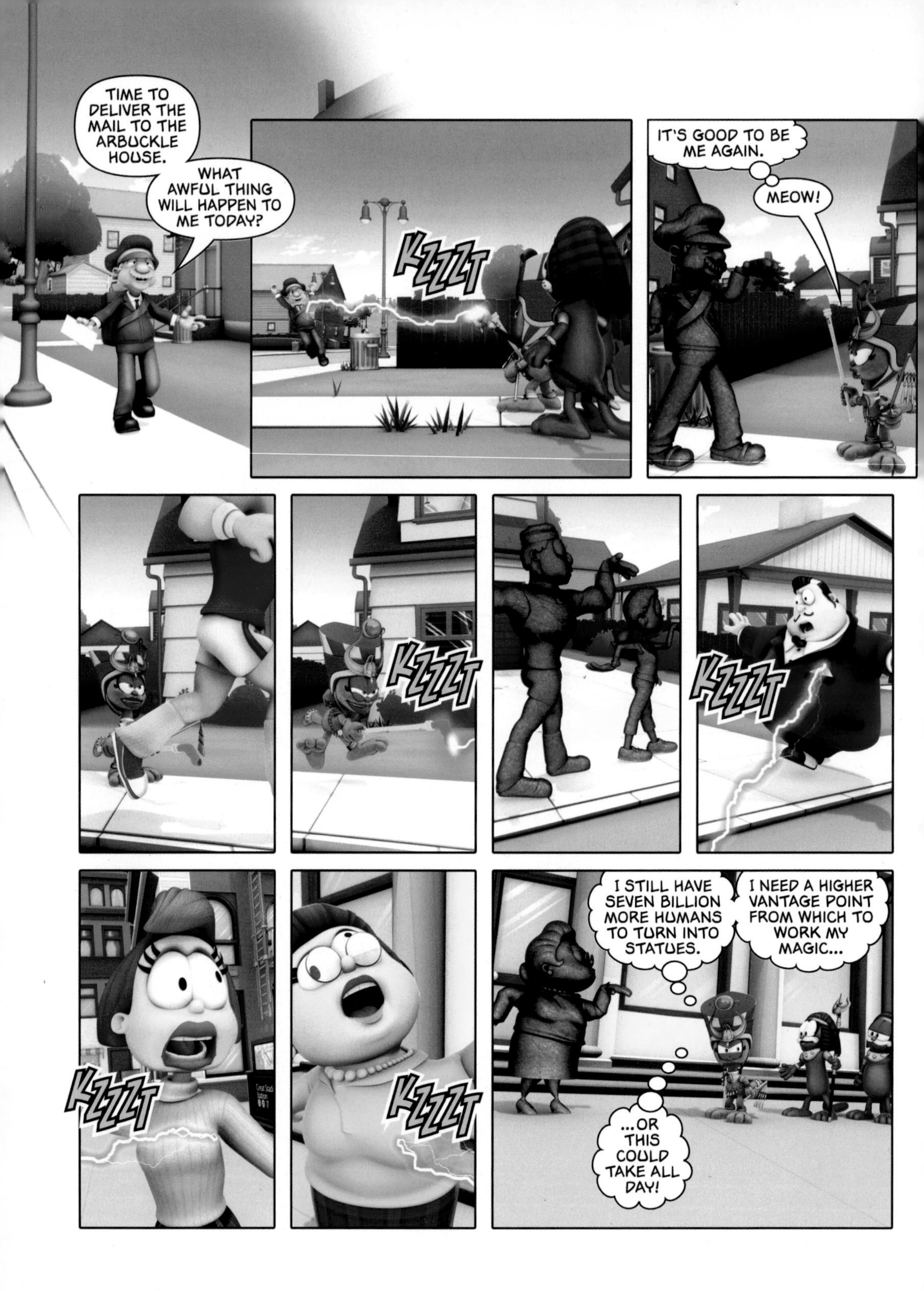
TIME TO DELIVER THE MAIL TO THE ARBUCKLE HOUSE.
WHAT AWFUL THING WILL HAPPEN TO ME TODAY?
KZZZT
IT'S GOOD TO BE ME AGAIN.
MEOW!
KZZZT
KZZZT
KZZZT
KZZZT
I STILL HAVE SEVEN BILLION MORE HUMANS TO TURN INTO STATUES.
I NEED A HIGHER VANTAGE POINT FROM WHICH TO WORK MY MAGIC...
...OR THIS COULD TAKE ALL DAY!

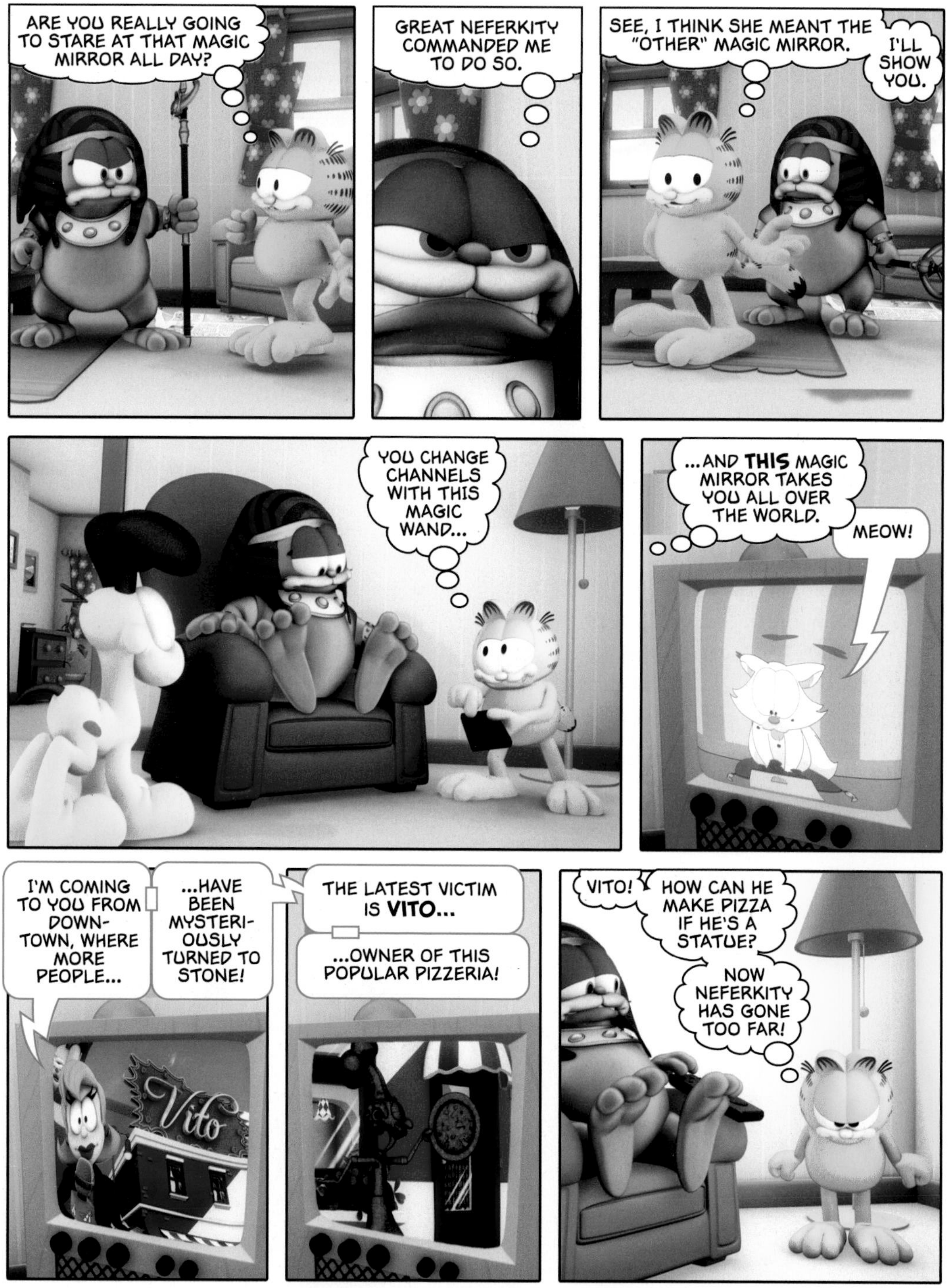
ARE YOU REALLY GOING TO STARE AT THAT MAGIC MIRROR ALL DAY?
GREAT NEFERKITY COMMANDED ME TO DO SO.
SEE, I THINK SHE MEANT THE "OTHER" MAGIC MIRROR.
I'LL SHOW YOU.
YOU CHANGE CHANNELS WITH THIS MAGIC WAND...
...AND THIS MAGIC MIRROR TAKES YOU ALL OVER THE WORLD.
MEOW!
I'M COMING TO YOU FROM DOWN-TOWN, WHERE MORE PEOPLE...
...HAVE BEEN MYSTERI-OUSLY TURNED TO STONE!
Vito
THE LATEST VICTIM IS VITO...
...OWNER OF THIS POPULAR PIZZERIA!
VITO!
HOW CAN HE MAKE PIZZA IF HE'S A STATUE?
NOW NEFERKITY HAS GONE TOO FAR!

Don't Miss THE GARFIELD SHOW #3 "Long Lost Lyman!"

Index of Terms

Carnivore: an animal that eats meat.

Coprolite: fossilized animal droppings.

Cretaceous: era between 145 and 65 million years ago.

Dinosaur: term created by Sir Richard Owen that means "fearfully great lizard." Dinosaurs were reptiles but had their own distinctive characteristics. (For example, they held their legs directly under their bodies.) All dinosaurs were land-based: none flew and none lived in the water.

Fossil: an animal or vegetable solidified in rock.

Herbivore: an animal that lives on plants. The term, "vegetarian," is probably more appropriate than "herbivore," as herbs and grass only appeared a little while after dinosaurs became extinct.

Jurassic: era between 200 and 145 million years ago.

Mammal: an animal with mammary glands, whose females nurse their young.

Ornithischian: a dinosaur with hips like a bird.

Paleontology: the science that studies extinct species. Its specialists are paleontologists.

Piscivore: an animal that eats fish.

Plesiosaur: a marine reptile that was almost a dinosaur.

Predator: an animal that attacks its prey to eat it.

Pterosaur: a flying reptile that was almost a dinosaur.

Reptiles: vertebrates that primarily crawl. They currently include crocodiles, lizards, snakes, turtles, and used to include dinosaurs, pterosaurs, and plesiosaurs.

Saurischian: a dinosaur with hips like a lizard.

Triassic: era in which dinosaurs appeared, between 250 and 200 million years ago.

GLOSSARY

Albertosaurus (Page 5)
Meaning: Alberta (Canadian Province) Lizard
Period: Late Cretaceous (70 million years ago)
Order/ Family: Saurischia/Tyrannosauridae
Size: 30 feet long
Weight: 6,000 lbs.
Diet: Carnivore
Found: North America

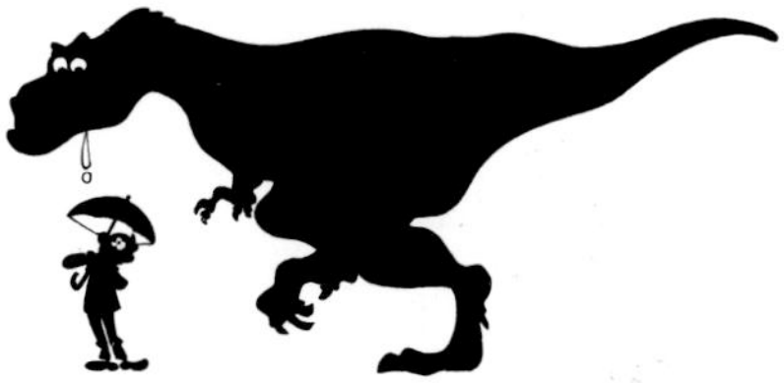

Bambiraptor (Page 18)
Meaning: Bambi Thief
Period: Late Cretaceous (80-72 million years ago)
Order/ Family: Saurischia/Dromaeosauridae
Size: 3 feet long
Weight: 5 lbs.
Diet: Carnivore
Found: North America

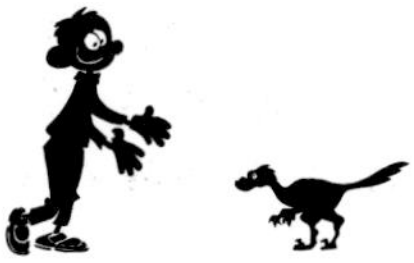

Baryonyx (Page 43)
Meaning: Heavy Claw
Period: Early Cretaceous (140-112 million years ago)
Order/ Family: Saurischia/Spinosauridae
Size: 33 feet long
Weight: 4,500 Lbs.
Diet: Piscivore and Carnivore
Found: England, Spain, and Portugal

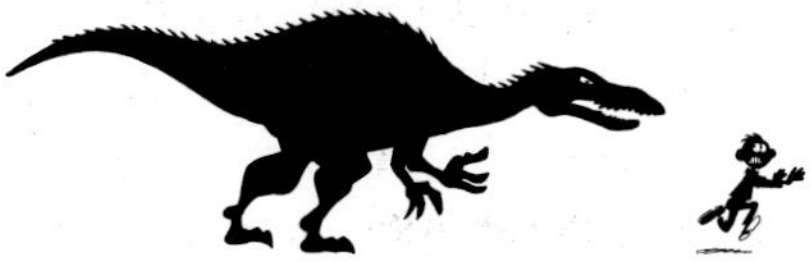

Camarasaurus (Page 34)
Meaning: Chambered Lizard
Period: Late Jurassic (155-144 million years ago)
Order/ Family: Saurischia/Camarasauridae
Size: 75 feet long
Weight: 60,000 lbs.
Diet: Herbivore
Found: North America

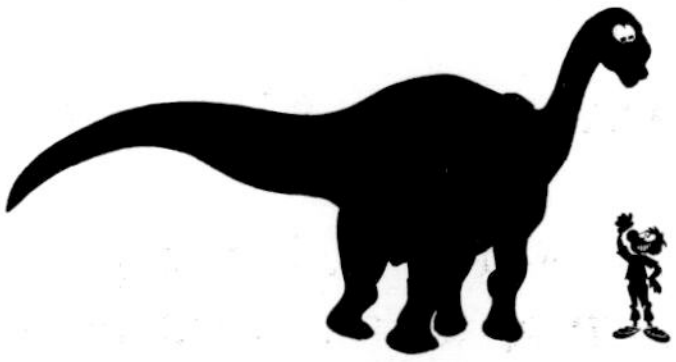

Carnotaurus (Page 12)
Meaning: Carnivorous Bull
Period: Late Cretaceous (83.5-65.5 million years ago)
Order/ Family: Saurischia/Abelisauridae
Size: 26 feet long
Weight: 3,300 lbs.
Diet: Carnivore
Found: South America

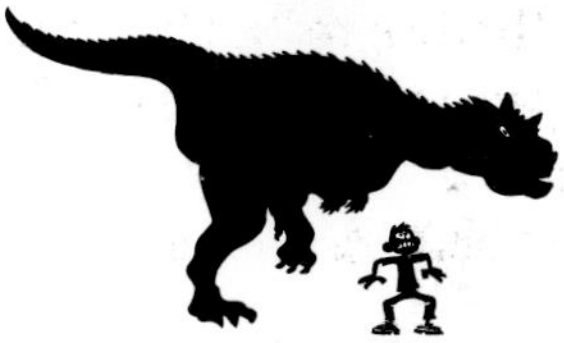

Concavenator Corcovatus (Page 37)
Meaning: Humpbacked Hunter from Cuenca
Period: Middle Jurassic (130 million years ago)
Order/ Family: Saurischia/Carcharodontosauridae
Size: 20 feet long
Weight: 4,400 lbs.
Diet: Carnivore
Found: Spain

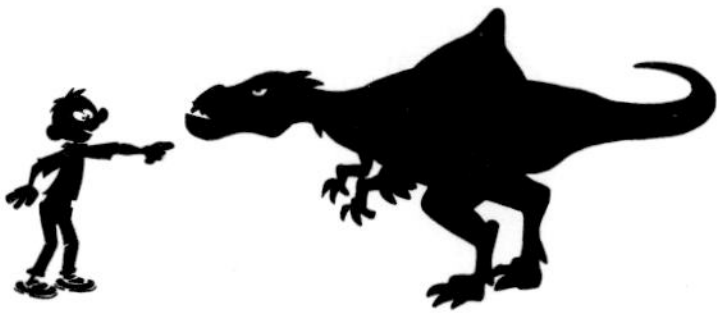

Deinocheirus (Page 44)
Meaning: Terrible Hand
Period: Late Cretaceous (70 million years ago)
Order/ Family: Saurischia/Deinocheiridae
Size: 35-50 feet long?
Weight: 4,400-11,000 lbs.?
Diet: Herbivore or Omnivore?
Found: Mongolia

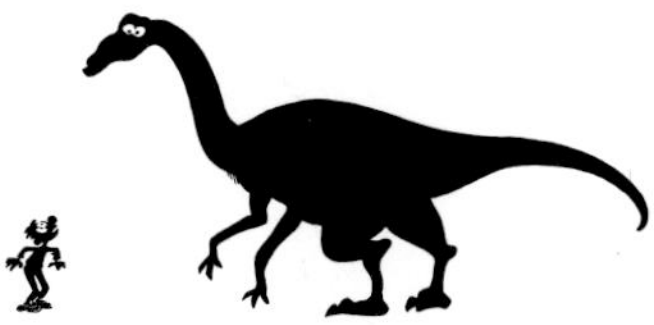

Dilophosaurus (Page 41)
Meaning: Two-Crested Lizard
Period: Early Jurassic (200-189 million years ago)
Order/ Family: Saurischia/Dilophosauridae
Size: 20 feet long
Weight: 1,100 lbs.
Diet: Carnivore
Found: North America, China

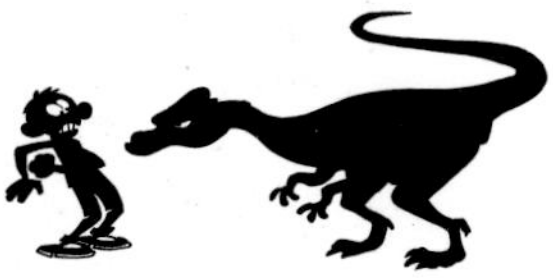

GLOSSARY

Euoplocephalus (Page 11)
Meaning: Well-Armed Head
Period: Late Cretaceous (80-66 million years ago)
Order/ Family: Ornithischia/Ankylosauridae
Size: 20 feet long
Weight: 4,400 lbs.
Diet: Herbivore
Found: North America

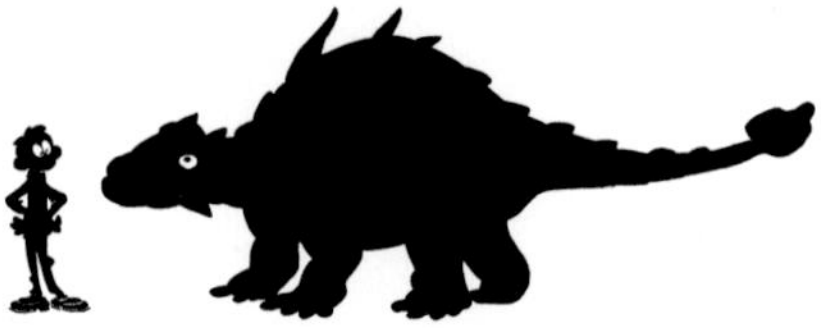

Gallimimus (Page 17)
Meaning: Chicken Mimic
Period: Late Cretaceous (75-70 million years ago)
Order/ Family: Saurischia/Orinthomimidae
Size: 20 feet long
Weight: 1,100 lbs.
Diet: Omnivore?
Found: Mongolia

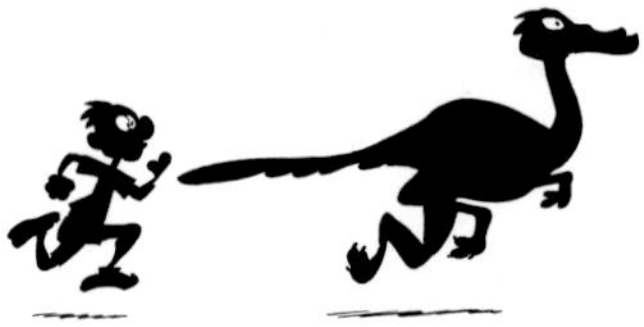

Maiasaura (Page 39)
Meaning: Caring Mother Lizard
Period: Late Cretaceous (80-72 million years ago)
Order/ Family: Ornithischia / Hadrosauridae
Size: 30 feet long
Weight: 6,600 lbs.
Diet: Herbivore?
Found: North America

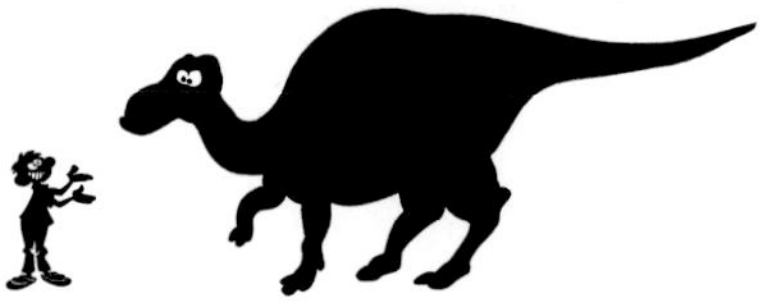

Psittacosaurus (Page 23)
Meaning: Parrot Lizard
Period: Early Cretaceous (130-100 million years ago)
Order/ Family: Orinthischia/Psittacosauridae
Size: 7 feet long
Weight: 44 lbs.
Diet: Herbivore
Found: China, Mongolia, Russia

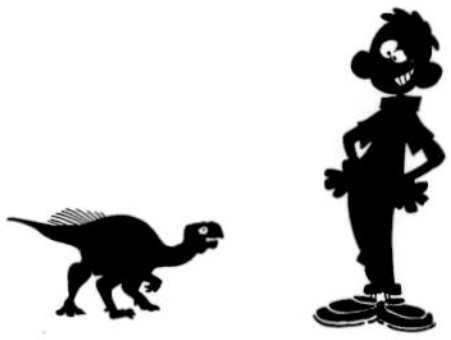

Quetzalcoatlus (Page 30)
Meaning: Named after the serpent god, Quetzal-coatl
Period: Late Cretaceous (70-65 million years ago)
Order/ Family: Pterosauria/Azhdarchidae
Size: 33 foot wingspan
Weight: 250 lbs.
Diet: Piscivore, Carnivore?
Found: North America

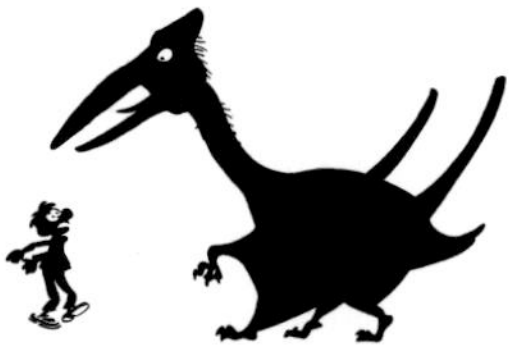

Saltasaurus (Page 20)
Meaning: Lizard from the Province of Salta
Period: Late Cretaceous (73-67 million years ago)
Order/ Family: Saurischia/Titanosauridae
Size: 40 feet long
Weight: 15,000 lbs.
Diet: Herbivore
Found: Argentina

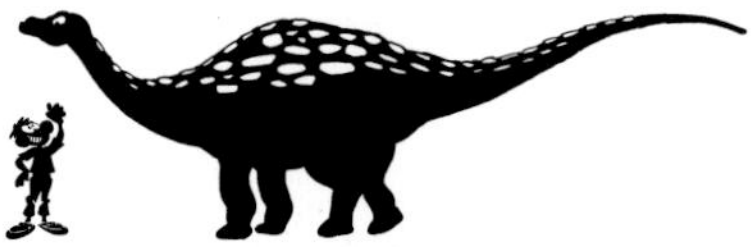

Spinosaurus (Page 29)
Meaning: Spiny Lizard
Period: Late Cretaceous (108-94 million years ago)
Order/ Family: Saurischia/Spinosauridae
Size: 50 feet long
Weight: 15,000 lbs.
Diet: Carnivore and Piscivore
Found: North Africa

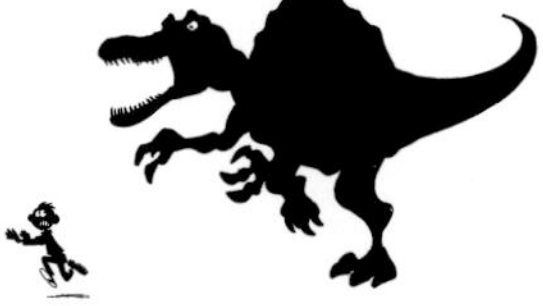

Therizinosaurus (Page 26)
Meaning: Scythe Lizard
Period: Late Cretaceous (70-65 million years ago)
Order/ Family: Saurischia/Therizinosauridae
Size: 30 feet long
Weight: 13,000 lbs.
Diet: Herbivore
Found: China, Mongolia

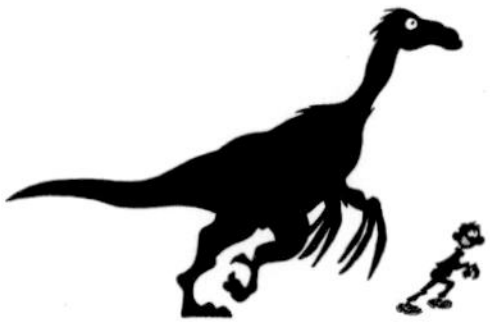

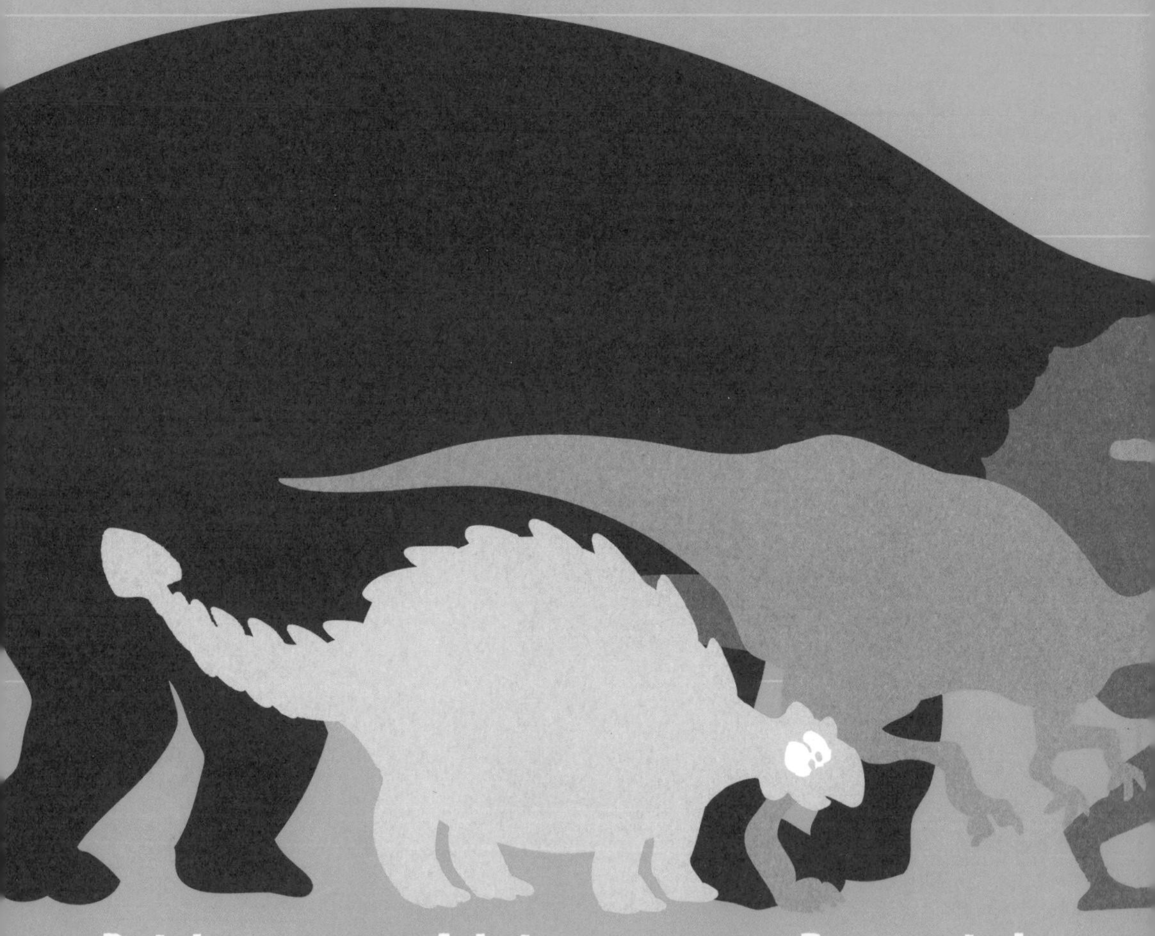
Diplodocus
Ankylosaurus
Parasaurolophus